THE SCARF

THE SCARF

A HICKORY LACE ADVENTURE

(Book 3 of The Prosperine Trilogy)

PJ McDermott

All characters and events in this publication, other than those clearly in the public domain, are fictitious and any resemblance to real persons, living or dead, is purely coincidental

List of Contents

Acknowledgements

To the members of my launch team, in particular Andrew Bernoth, Gale Canzoneri, Mandy Waldken-Brown, Nina Light, Richard Meek, and Tara Campbell, thank you for your support and encouragement.

"Through the ages, until proven otherwise, we have considered ourselves to be the center of the universe. There is really no reason to believe humanity is the sole creation in God's image."

Pope Innocent XIV, 2086–2105

PROSPERINE

One: Temloki

Temloki's leathery wings rippled in the blustery breeze, rousing him momentarily from his slumber. The journey from Avanaux had been long and arduous, and the sword grew more burdensome with each passing hour. His strength would not last forever, he knew, but it would suffice until he reached his destination. *The Scarf.* He quivered with excitement in his half-sleep. At last, he would be with his kinfolk.

He'd nested alone these past three hundred years, ever since that dire day Ka-Varla had failed to return from the hunt. He'd woken with her screams echoing through his dreams and immediately left the lair to search for his mate. Temloki tracked her to the marshlands outside the city of Crodal.

There, amongst the white water lilies, he discovered Ka-Varla near death. She lay on her side, pierced by a score of arrows, with thick black blood oozing from her belly, swollen with the nymphlet she'd carried these last eighteen months. She lifted her head and keened as he approached. Temloki dripped water into her mouth and brought her fresh meat until she could no longer swallow. Her breathing became weaker and more labored, and finally, it ceased with a sigh. He remained with her until long after she'd grown cold.

Temloki grieved many months for the loss of his mate. She'd been with him near a century, the mother of four nymphlets, all of them dead at the hands of the wingless ones. Each night before they slept, they relived the joy of the chase and the kill, and shared their bewilderment over the endless wars between the six kingdoms of Erlach.

Ka-Varla and Temloki were the last of their kind on the northern continent, and after his mate's passing, Temloki lived in solitude, emerging from his cave only to hunt, his sorrow and hurt souring to anger and hate. The rage festered inside him day by day until all thoughts but those of revenge fled his mind.

He brought terror to the wingless ones, the Erlachi, demanding they give him their children, their mates, as they had taken his. His revenge knew no limit. Many of his victims he swallowed whole to satisfy his hunger, but others he tore apart slowly for the pleasure of watching them die. His appearance at the gates of any city created hysteria amongst the population and earned him his epithet, Riv-Amok, 'bringer of death.'

And in two hundred years he had never heard another voice until the warrior from the stars whispered in his mind. At first, he thought he dreamed again of Ka-Varla, then with mounting excitement, he hoped the whisperer might perhaps be one of his own, miraculously come from a far country to seek him out. But hope turned to bitterness when he realized the stranger was nothing but a wingless warrior. He sought her out, but her will was strong, and she evaded him. In the end, he devoured two of her companions before the White One commanded him to leave and take the sword to the Scarf.

In the first days of his journey, he fancied he'd heard the weapon murmur to him, urging him forward with promises of great treasures, but he laughed at it. Nothing created by the hand of a wingless one could hold sway over him.

Temloki grasped the sword more firmly in his talons and coasted lower, cocking his head to survey his new home: a hot and steamy place with salt-encrusted white rock cracked and broken into a million pieces by rivulets of seawater, and seemingly devoid of life. There was nothing for him here. He groaned, but beat his massive wings and flew on.

The sun sank beneath the sea, and the planet Prosperine's two orange-dusted moons rose high. The aurora unfolded like a curtain, and the sky was blanketed with pulsating sheets of emerald, ruby, and turquoise. A thin ribbon of gold rippled slowly across the heavens and sank beneath the horizon. Temloki cared naught for this natural beauty and fastened his eyes on the land below.

Gradually the terrain changed. Occasional patches of lichen and algae joined together, and the salted crust gave way to rushes and ferns and then to swamps infested with biting insects and creeping plants. Bushes and scrubby trees emerged, growing taller by consuming their own branches, leaf litter, and the occasional dead animal. The land rose in places, forming hillocks and ridges in the otherwise flat vastness.

A flicker of light caught his eye, and Temloki turned towards it, his heart suddenly aflame.

Two: Trouble in the Scarf

Admiral George Lace, Earth representative at the Intragalactic Agency, stared at his adopted daughter, his fingers tapping the table between them. "You're telling me this sword has magical powers that enhance the strength of whoever happens to own it?"

Hickory squirmed in her seat. She was aboard the admiral's flagship, the Jabberwocky, being debriefed on her recent assignment to Erlach. She found it hard to accept this man as her father, preferring to think of him as the Admiral, with a capital "A." After her mother died giving birth to her younger brother, he'd offloaded both of them to his sister, Maddie. For ten years, the only communication Hickory received from him was an occasional birthday card with his name printed on it. In the last five years, there'd been nothing. Then, out of the blue, she'd been transferred from the Alien Corps to work with him on a mission to Prosperine.

Hickory was a neoteric, one of a small percentage

of the population born with nascent empathic ability, a rare mutation that emerged during the Dark Age following World War III. As a result of this, she could sense the emotions of others and tell when someone lied or distorted the truth by reaching out to them with her mind.

She knew the admiral scorned anything that hinted of the paranormal. She spread her hands wide. "I don't say *magic*, sir. Sequana's strength could have been coincidental, but the Sword of Connat-sèra-Haagar affected his mind. Those who knew him say his whole personality changed in the weeks before I killed him. He remained a charismatic leader of the rebellion and a brilliant thinker much loved by his followers, even after his defeat. Then, a few months after acquiring the sword, he became paranoid and suspicious of everyone around him. I believe the sword helped Sequana to become powerful, but in the end, it also made him vulnerable. The legends of the Avanauri say that the sword magnifies weaknesses as well as strengths."

The admiral snorted, then changed tack. "And you lost this weapon? You had it in your hand, yet you lost it?"

Hickory nodded carefully. She didn't want to lie to the admiral, but she didn't want him to know the truth—that Gareth, her sidekick, had given the Sword of Connat-sèra-Haagar to the Avanauri mystic called the Teacher, who in turn had placed it in the keeping of the ferocious telepathic creature, the Riv-Amok. "I have an idea where it might be, though. I heard someone say it was taken to the Scarf for safe keeping."

"Someone?" The admiral laughed. "And who would that *someone* be, I wonder? Never mind." He raised his hand. "I don't want lies, and in any case, if it's in the Scarf, it may not be so safe as you think." He shook his head. "I don't know how Yonni is going to take this. He desperately wants that sword back."

Hickory's eyes flashed. The admiral had made a pact with Avanaux's ruler, Yonni-sèr-Abelen, to bring him the sword in exchange for a license to mine crynidium, a vital ingredient in the fuel that enabled FTL travel. The liquid metal had been discovered on only a handful of planets, and the IA was desperate to secure the long-term rights on Prosperine. Hickory suspected that part of the deal also involved getting rid of the Teacher whom Yonni believed to be a threat to his authority.

Hickory had been seconded from the Alien Corps to retrieve the fabled weapon when Sequana had stolen it from the temple. In the end, she had decided that Prosperine and its people were better served if the sword remained hidden.

"I understood the Scarf to be uninhabited," she said.

The admiral's eyes fixed on hers, but he said nothing.

Hickory poured water into her glass and sipped at it. "The ship's vids describe it as a barren place—mostly swamp and jungle. The only things that live there are flies, spiders and a bunch of other squishy creepy-crawlies." She shivered. "I would have thought it the perfect place to lose anything for a few thousand years."

The admiral's chair scraped across the floor, and he walked to the viewscreen where the planet Prosperine shone like a blue and red jewel swathed in white clouds. "Our initial exploration of the Scarf may have been a *little* less than thorough." He darted a glance at Hickory. "When our first flyby indicated no sentient life there, I made a decision not to expend resources exploring the area. Later analysis of the data showed that higher life forms do in fact exist—on some of the islands, at least.

"I decided to run another scan, and we picked up signals indicating the presence of small bipedal populations. We think they may be nocturnal cave-dwellers, which would explain why we didn't find them on our first scan. So far, we've located six groups of between two and three hundred each. We can't get more detail because the radiation in that area is pretty bad and it interferes with our scanning." He laughed with a short bark. "Given what you've just told me, though, I don't have any alternative. I'm going to have to send a team down there to look around."

If there was one thing Hickory didn't want to do ever again, it was to go into a jungle—any jungle. She recalled her mission two years back on Aquarius Four. For six months, there'd been tropical rain, leeches, and carnivorous plants to deal with. She'd hated it, but she could have coped if she hadn't gone against all her training and allowed herself to become romantically involved with one of the crew.

An anonymous well-wisher sent her a note saying Jacob had been married for seven years. The ensuing break up was vitriolic, and she'd lost her focus on the operation. To top it off, her main quarry had been assassinated under her nose.

When she returned to Earth, emotionally and physically exhausted, her boss, Prefect Cortherien, had dismissed her from active service and transferred her to a job teaching at the Saint Philip Research Academy—the training ground for the Alien Corps.

The admiral's eyes locked on hers. "I know you have issues with working in these sort of conditions, and if you don't want to go, I'll find someone else."

A tear came unexpectedly to her eye. *He's trying to manipulate me.* She was nothing more than a pawn to this man who called himself her father, a pawn he would have no hesitation in sacrificing to achieve his own ends. She'd been on the planet twice in the last six months masquerading as one of the natives. If she undertook the maquillage treatment one more time, she'd have to return to Earth for re-humanizing. That would be a particularly unpleasant experience—not that he cared. She blinked the moisture away. "That's what you'd better do, then. I've had enough of adventure for a while."

*

Hickory sipped at her glass of Barbaresco and flicked the hollo-channel over to classical. She selected the Slovak National Philharmonic Orchestra's rendition of *Rhapsody in Blue*. The quirky mix of classical and jazz elements perfectly reflected her conflicting emotions. She'd been back on Earth for two weeks, eating at the best restaurants, attending recitals and stage shows and catching up with Jess, Mack, Gareth, and Jenny.

It was great to see how happy they all were, and how very much in love and unafraid to express their affections in public they'd all become. *There*. The pang of envy, or was it self-pity, seared her heart, and she wondered if she would ever find a soul mate. She shook her head. Such is life. The affair with Jacob had been nothing more than a fling.

The nearest she'd come to being in love had been with Kar-sèr-Sephiryth, the alien known as the Teacher, on her last mission to Prosperine. But that was different, wasn't it? She was attracted by his gentleness, his compassion, his selflessness. She felt safe in his company, and if he had been human, she might have fallen head over heels.

She shook her head, tutting at her self-delusion. *God, I'm a moron. Every time I see him, I feel a wild impulse to wrap my arms around him.* Kar was the most exciting, mysterious person she'd ever come across, and perhaps something more.

The Alien Corps had searched the galaxy for signs of the Messiah ever since the discovery of an ancient manuscript in 2095 prophesied that he would appear on an alien planet at the end of days.

Cortherien had reinstated Hickory as a commander in the Corps specifically to discover the truth about the Teacher. The report she'd provided to the Prefect concluded Kar-sèr-Sephiryth represented an early manifestation of a predicted leap in the evolution of the Avanauri species. She still wasn't sure if this was the case, but Kar was no more attainable to her than if he'd turned out to be the reincarnation of the Christ.

She sighed. How badly did she need to get a life? Mooning over an *alien*.

The holo-screen beeped to signal an incoming message. Hickory checked the identity of the caller. The Admiral. She pushed her glass to one side, straightened her collar and accepted the call.

"Hickory! How are you? Enjoying your vacation?"

"Sir, you didn't call to check whether I'm having a relaxing time."

He shook his head and smiled. "Always the same mistrustful daughter, desperate to get straight to the point. Would it kill you to be pleasant to your father for a change?"

She maintained a blank expression with difficulty. The admiral wasn't her birth father and, considering his indifference to her over the years, their relationship was anything but familial. She knew it, and he knew it, but he wasn't beyond playing the family ties card to get what he wanted. She hated that. "What do you want?" she said.

"Alright, have it your way." He gave a curt nod. "There's been a development on Prosperine. After you decided not to help, I sent a team into the Scarf to look around. They've disappeared."

Hickory's eyebrows rose. "What happened?"

"I don't know. We lost track shortly after the pilot reported seeing a crashed jet."

A shadow crossed Hickory's heart. "What kind of jet?"

"Bikashi."

Hickory felt the heat rise up her neck. The Teacher's last words before she left Erlach sprang to mind: *Something stirs in the Scarf. I fear the sword is no longer silent.*

"There's Bikashi in the Scarf?" The Bikashi, a warlike species, had once been members of the IA. They'd been thrown out after several attempts to defraud the other representatives. On her first mission, a squad of Bikashi troops had joined forces with Sequana and his Avanauri rebels, intent on seizing the planet's stocks of crynidium.

"I can't say for certain. Brox didn't report seeing any on his fly past, and unfortunately, he went off-air soon after. Rescue are out there now looking for our people. But we can't take the risk." He paused. "Hickory, they could be after the sword."

Hickory snorted. "Even if they knew about the sword, how would they know to look in the Scarf? Surely it's a coincidence? You don't *know* how long they've been there. They might have crashed years ago."

"Perhaps," said the admiral. "But I can't afford to take the chance of someone like Vogel getting their hands on it."

"Vogel! You don't think he's in the Scarf?" The commander of the Bikashi Shock Pack had kidnapped and tortured Gareth on their first trip to Prosperine. The Teacher had done what he was able to heal the boy, but some of the emotional scars remained with him.

"Just putting two and two together. We know he

escaped after the battle of Ezekan, but we never heard of him after that. It may not be him."

"Sounds like a long shot." But if there stood a remote chance of it being Vogel, the admiral couldn't afford to ignore it. She swallowed hard. "Admiral, I can't go back to Prosperine, not to the Scarf. I'm sorry, you'll have to find someone else."

"Oh I know, Hickory. I didn't expect you to. I've found someone who's keen to do the job. I just called to let you know that Gareth Blanquette is on his way here."

Hickory's head swirled: if there were any chance of him getting a chance to exact revenge on Vogel, Gareth would indeed be more than eager to go.

*

Hickory and Jess sat at a table outside the Cafe Dolce in Rome. They'd ordered pasta for lunch, but neither felt like eating. "Sometimes that boy is as thick as two bricks, genius or not," said Jess, her eyes afire. "He didn't say a word to me."

"Because he knew you'd try to stop him going— the same as I would, that's why. It's too late to be angry, Jess, he's half way to Prosperine by now."

"The admiral's bullying you into this, you know that don't you? You don't have to go. Gareth's a big boy now." Jess pushed some gnocchi around her plate with her fork. "Do you think it's Vogel?" She gave Hickory a sidelong glance.

"I'm *afraid* it is. And if so, losing Gareth isn't the only problem we'll have. If the Bikashi gets his hands on the sword, God knows what he'll be capable of."

"So, you're going?" Jess nudged her plate into the middle of the table.

Hickory raised an eyebrow and smiled wryly. "Much as I wish I didn't have to, I don't feel there's any option. I've asked the admiral to keep Gareth in cold storage until I arrive."

Jess folded her arms. "Until *we* arrive."

Three: Bikashi

Vogel's long snout twitched as he slammed the micro-solder down on the comms panel. Broad and tall, even for a Bikashi, his head resembled an enormous soft-shelled turtle, and his body was covered in micro-scales. He hissed through the thin, ragged slit of his mouth. *Shrelek!* Another wasted morning. The ship was obviously beyond repair. The FTL drive appeared unharmed, but unless he could get her off the ground he'd never know for sure. He glanced out the doorway and across the swampland to where his soldiers sat playing cards. They were no help. They'd given up any hope of getting off this planet a long time ago. He glared at them. If they ever managed to return to Auriga, he'd have the lot of them flogged and then the skin flayed from their flesh an inch at a time. He should kill them now, but useless and undisciplined as they were, they were still Bikashi, his own people. In truth, it had been harder on them than he—at least his personal radiation shield had survived the crash. The

Prosperine sun hadn't been merciful to his troops. Typically hard and toughened like cracked basalt, their exposed flesh was now covered in red welts. Without doubt, they'd be dead in a few months, even if they escaped from this planet.

Vogel jumped from the ship onto the squelchy bed of reeds and vines that supported the space-fighter. They'd been first-rate soldiers once, the finest in the Bikashi army, but that was before they were routed at Ezekan, forced to flee from the marauding Charakai. As a reflex, his eyes darted skyward. He shivered as he recalled being pursued by the reptile-birds, snapping at his neck and screeching in frenzy. The raised voices of his soldiers chased away his meandering thoughts.

Revlek, his lieutenant, was running towards him leaping across half submerged creepers while pointing to the sky. He called out to his commander, jabbering in his excitement.

Vogel turned and shaded his eyes. He frowned. Something, a seabird perhaps, flew high overhead. He watched as it banked towards them, growing bigger by the second. No, not a bird; it was a reptile of sorts, by the look of its membrane wings and elongated head, but much bigger than the vicious Charakai that plagued his sleep. He drew his blaster and checked the gauge, even though he knew the load was almost depleted. At most, he had two decent shots left. He started towards the thick forest two hundred yards away, shouting, "Revlek, get those *craiks* into cover. Now!"

Revlek drew his sword and urged the four Bikashi across the swamp. Seized by panic, they bumped into each other, stumbling as they ran. One of the warriors glanced over his shoulder and tripped on a vine. He fell through a break in the vegetation and disappeared into the murky water below.

Vogel sprinted to the scene, but there was no sign of the missing soldier. He kicked at the water, cursed, then resumed his flight, bounding over the swampland and crashing through the scrub to join his remaining troops.

The Riv-Amok circled the spaceship several times before it landed on a firm patch of reedy tussocks. It stretched its neck, shook its massive leathery wings, then folded them close to its body.

Crouched behind cover at the edge of the forest, a soldier nodded at the weapon clutched in the beast's claw and whispered to his comrade, "What magic is this, that a creature wields a sword?"

The Riv-Amok's head snapped towards the Bikashi, its long beak hovering barely inches above the swamp. It dropped the sword on the matted vines and crept stealthily towards the trees, stopping every few yards to listen.

Vogel motioned with his gun for his troops to

move further into the forest. A branch snapped beneath Revlek's foot, sounding like a crack of thunder in the still air.

The creature opened its beak and emitted a shrill shriek.

The sound terrified the Bikashi troops, and they bolted, careless of the noise they made. Vogel's eyes grew wide, but he remained crouched, still and silent, his attention fixed on the approaching monster.

The Riv-Amok crashed through the trees, its great wings snapping them like matchsticks and its clawed feet tearing bushes up by the roots. The Bikashi broke in four different directions, but the beast was too quick for them. One by one, it plucked the weakened soldiers from their surroundings, tossed them into the air and swallowed them whole. The beast's throat bulged grotesquely whenever a Bikashi soldier slid down its gullet.

Vogel watched horrified from his hiding place in the hollow of a large tree. He saw Revlek, the last of his crew, dash out of the forest and make a dash for the ship. Leaping over gaps in the ground cover and skirting larger pools of open water, he had almost made it when the monster pounced. Revlek screamed as a great claw pinned him to the ground and the beast devoured strips of flesh from his still conscious body. With a cry of triumphant joy, the Riv-Amok silenced him, tearing his head from his body.

When it finished eating, the creature settled on its belly and licked the blood from its claws. Then it rose and sniffed the air. It reentered the forest, less than twenty yards from where Vogel crouched.

Cold sweat broke out on the back of the Bikashi commander's neck. He tore his eyes away from the monstrosity and pushed himself as far back into the tree hollow as he could go.

Should he try to run? If he could get to the ship, he might survive—though he didn't doubt the monster had the strength to rip the hull apart. He felt something wet ooze onto his head and crawl down his neck onto his shoulder. He ignored the slimy insect, keeping his eyes fixed on the creature. Its back was turned, about fifty yards away. He crept out of the tree hollow and shook the bug from his hand, then crawled on his belly to the forest's edge. He noticed the sword lying where the creature had left it, about half-way to the ship. One last glance over his shoulder to make sure the monster hadn't spotted him and Vogel ran. He scooped up the weapon on his way past, then scrambled through the ship's doorway.

The monster's screams followed him inside. Vogel sucked in his breath as the Riv-Amok emerged from the trees and launched itself at the spacecraft, half flying, half running, its claws spraying water. The Bikashi commander scrambled away from the doorway just as the monster's head probed the opening, dripping blood and gore. It opened its jaws and filled the cabin with its shriek and the stench of death.

A faint echo of the beast's cry sounded from outside the ship. It withdrew its head and turned to the west. The sound came again, and the monster shrieked an answer. Taking a last malevolent look towards the ship, the Riv-Amok skimmed across the clearing, unfolded its wings and launched itself into the air.

*

Vogel staggered outside, placed his hands on his knees and vomited. He brushed his mouth roughly on the back of his sleeve and glanced around. Revlek's helmet, with his head inside, lay just this side of the trees. Vogel searched, but little other than the dark blood and a few severed limbs indicated the Bikashi had ever been there.

He slumped to his knees and buried his head in his hands. Ten minutes before, he had been planning to have them executed, tortured as their reward for letting him down. Now, all Vogel could think of was what they'd once been and how proud he'd felt to be their leader.

He stared at the sword he had captured. Strange the creature would carry such a thing. Perhaps it had been attracted to the shiny metal. He scratched at an itch on his leg. He was alone now. But he felt thankful to be alive, even if life had been reduced to the most basic level in this *Herek*-forsaken land.

He rubbed at his cheek absently. He'd have to forage more widely for food. His troops had just about hunted the surrounding area to extinction. Animal life was scarce anyway in the Scarf, but fish were plentiful in the nearby lagoons—strange, brightly colored swimmers with legs as well as fins, and eyes that looked unsettlingly intelligent. It caused his stomach to churn when one of the bigger ones had been set on the fire to cook. Its eyes had turned to his, and he'd decided that he would eat them no longer. His soldiers hadn't shown the same scruples. He rubbed his head, then scratched at his crotch. *What the—?* He stood up and brushed at his clothes. Tiny insects covered him. They had burrowed under his clothes and into his hair, and they bit.

Vogel ran back to the ship, his arms flailing. He flicked on the purification system and stripped off his clothes. Hot water from the lagoon delivered via a crude but effective pipe system steamed forth and scoured his skin. He lathered soap into the small patch of hair on his head and scrubbed his body until it hurt. He stayed under the shower a long time, letting the warmth penetrate and soothe.

Afterward, the commander put on a fresh set of underclothes and his alternate uniform and then readjusted his radiation protection. He would miss the small comforts afforded by the ship when he moved on, but he wouldn't survive in this swamp much longer. He picked up the sword absently and stared at it. *Where did you come from, I wonder?* The long blade gleamed brightly. Avanauri weaponsmiths sometimes fused crynidium to the steel to improve its sharpness and durability. He heaved the sword in his hand, surprised at how light it felt. He swung it back and forth in a series of Bikashi training routines, and it felt almost as though the sword anticipated his moves and led his hand.

Vogel placed the blade in the corner of the ship where he could keep his eyes on it and mixed himself a glass of Shirezan. The Bikashi liqueur was standard issue on every ship from his home planet, Auriga. This was the last bottle. He settled himself into a chair and sighed. As he sipped the drink appreciatively, the Bikashi commander's eyes sought the sword time and again. Eventually, he retrieved the weapon and laid it across his knees. Recent events and the bleak future that stretched ahead made him weary. Tiredness overcame him, his head drooped onto his chest, and he fell into a deep sleep.

*

Connat-sèra-Haagar sat astride the massive yarrak, her body encased in chain mail and an armored helm upon her head. Despite the bulky protection, she felt light of heart and filled with energy as she watched the Erlachi hordes approach. She'd waited for this day. Tensions had been building between the two neighboring states over sovereignty of the border for almost a year. When a party of Avanauri farmers decided to settle the land around Crodal, Erlach's patience snapped. The Erlachi army slaughtered one hundred and twenty naurs and nauris and then marched south.

They were many, come to Ezekan to kill and enslave her people in the name of the one God, Balor. Connat spat. Both countries believed in the same God but would happily slay innocents as well as other believers in his name. Her glance took in the city guard stretched out in a sparse front to either side of her. They looked nervous, undecided whether to run or fight. She could sense they were almost resolved to surrender.

Since the sword had chosen her to be its champion, the young nauri's sensitivity to the thoughts and emotions of those around her had flourished. Oftentimes, she understood what others were thinking and sensed what they were about to do even before they, themselves, knew. This was one of many changes wrought by the sword. Connat's strength was unequaled in Avanaux, and her skill with any weapon such that none could stand against her. She had also developed an insatiable thirst for knowledge. Rarely did she feel the need for sleep, spending each night reading books and scrolls when all others had gone to bed. She'd studied every tome in the city library, a small building to look at, but one that held the priceless, written wealth of the nation, and she had journeyed far seeking to learn more.

The more wisdom she absorbed, the stronger grew the bond between her and the sword. The stronger the bond, the more its power flowed through her.

These wonders came at a price. Her family could not comprehend the extraordinary warrior she had become, and they shunned her. Friends she had grown up with feared to come near lest they be consumed by the strange lights dancing in her eyes. Contrarily, strangers idolized her and left her little privacy. An object of awe and veneration among the Avanauri common people, Connat-sèra-Haagar drew attention everywhere she went. The lack of close friendships meant little to her, and she knew this was also part of the change the sword had wrought in her.

She struggled to remain faithful to the person she had been before the sword claimed her, cultivating a strict regimen of exercise, meditation, and prayer. She succeeded at least partly in retaining a vestige of the farm girl she had once been, hunting wild loopas with her friends in the woods and sitting at her father's hearth listening to tales of the magical folk, the Lonilki.

But today, Connat knew it would be different. The enemy would come amongst them, and she would turn the power of the sword loose. She prayed to Balor for the strength to regain her mortality when the day was done.

She pulled on the reigns of the yarrack so that it reared high, then raised the sword and let the Avanauri and the Erlachi alike glimpse its power as it flared bright in the light of the sun. "Ayeiii!" she screamed. "Today is a day to fight. Today is a day to maim and kill. For if we, the chosen ones of Balor, do not vanquish the barbarians, they will surely lay waste to our homes and murder and mutilate our families. Follow the sword, Avanauri, and it will lead you to victory!"

A roar of approval from the ranks was met by calls of derision and jeering from the assembled Erlachi. Connat urged her yarrak into a gallop towards the enemy. Hundreds of fighting naurs and nauris holding pikes and banners followed her and crashed into their adversaries. Yarraks and Perines alike shrieked with the lust for battle.

Connat swept the sword in a circle above her head and, uttering a primal scream, she scythed into the enemy. The Erlachi warriors facing her threw down their swords and crawled under the feet of yarraks in their desperation to escape. Others turned to flee but were pressed close by those behind. Every swing of the sword separated half a dozen heads from their bodies. Many others lost limbs or suffered wounds to their chest and stomach. All the while, Connat controlled the movement of her steed with her knees and an occasional mental order to veer right or left. She sliced into the ranks of the enemy and swept out the other side. She turned time and time again, shredding the might of the Erlachi army so that her own troops found it an easy task to mop up the remnants. Occasionally, an arrow found its target but glanced harmlessly off her armor. No swordsman came within striking distance of the furious berserker.

*

Vogel woke abruptly, his heart hammering. Shafts of daylight poured through the open cabin door, temporarily disorienting him. He shook his head. The dream had been spectacularly vivid, real. He could still feel the astonishing power of the sword coursing through him; hear the anguished screams of the fallen; smell the blood of the victims and feel the exultation as he routed their forces. He had been as one with the female warrior, sharing her blood lust, her struggles to remain Avanauri in the midst of her excesses, her exhilaration, and her regrets. Connat-sèra-Haagar. The name came to him easily—the legendary Avanauri heroine who had been responsible for the defeat of the Erlachi thousands of years earlier.

What had brought this long dead general into his subconscious? After all, he had only passing knowledge of this legend from the mists of time. Perhaps the devastation caused by the giant flying reptile had affected his mind more than he realized.

The sword lay on his lap where he'd placed it. He brought it close, examining the weapon in detail for the first time. It looked identical to the one Connat had wielded: long, double-edged and shining, with a distinct hand-guard encrusted with multicolored gems and molded in the shape of a bird of prey. He ran his fingers across a row of faded symbols inscribed on the hilt, almost erased by time. In his dream, the sword possessed an incredible power. The heroine had been a vessel; at least partly an unwilling one, but a channel through which the sword worked its magic.

Abruptly, Vogel went outside. He gathered twigs and tree branches from the forest's edge and built a fire on top of the hillock where the winged monster had landed. He added more fuel until the interior glowed white and blue. The commander searched the ship for a hammer and selected half a dozen metal rods from the wreckage. He heated the rods until they were yellow-orange, then fashioned a rough scabbard for the sword. He would wear it on his belt. The makeshift holder would prevent the sharp blade from cutting into his leg. He tested out the combination and was pleased with the result.

Vogel considered his position. No one knew of his whereabouts, so it was unlikely anyone would arrive to rescue him. The communications panel was beyond repair, meaning he couldn't send a distress signal. Indeed, little of value could be salvaged from the ship. It seemed pointless to him to hang around now that his companions were dead. He wondered what manner of monster had killed them. He'd never seen the like of it, on this planet or any other. Perhaps it was indigenous to the Scarf. Why had it carried a sword, and one so finely crafted as this? Could there be a connection between his dream and the winged creature? He pondered these mysteries for a few minutes but came up with no satisfactory answers. He shrugged. The beast must be involved in some way.

He gazed across the inlet at the island with the strangely shaped mountain. It looked only a few miles away. The monster had left in that direction. Vogel decided to search the island for the creature and hope he would find answers before he killed it. He bore the monster no grudge: it was a wild animal; the slaughter of his men had been instinctive. The creature could bear no malice. But it was a matter of honor for him. His soldiers' deaths must be avenged. This would be a fitting final quest to end his life.

He went back to the spaceship and bundled up the remaining food, water, spare clothes, an extra pair of boots and a variety of tools, and looked around one last time. He picked up his blaster, then threw it back on the couch. No point in bringing useless junk. It would only slow him down.

Four: "I Hate Jungle"

"**H**old on to your hats, boys and girls. We're about to elevator-drop straight through the ionosphere," said Jess Parker whooping gleefully. She could have put the drive into auto, but Jess loved the adrenalin rush from being in control of the ship.

Hickory glanced at the four passengers. Most of them had their eyes shut and were clinging fiercely to the arms of their seats as the ship bounced and shuddered. None were recognizable as Earthlings, as their physical appearance had been transformed by the maquillage process to mimic the main species of the planet Prosperine.

Modern Avanauri were humanoid, but a few features from their distant origins were still evident. Descended from warm-blooded egg-laying vertebrates with traits similar to Earth's extinct herbivorous dinosaurs, the males and females of the species—the naurs and nauris—were hairless except for their eyebrows and a strip running across their skull that stretched from the forehead to halfway down the spine. Their pupils were large and shockingly blue, and the females displayed prominently sculptured cheekbones. The most striking differences between naurs and nauris, however, were also evident amongst the transformed humans. Whereas the males had black pigmentation around their eyes, Hickory's and Jess's skin shone with speckled purple markings that began at their eyes and followed the curvature of their cheekbones to fade at their earlobes.

All IA personnel assigned to Prosperine underwent the same transformation process. The measures had been agreed between the IA and the Avanauri government to prevent panic amongst the superstitious medieval inhabitants who had no knowledge that aliens walked amongst them.

While the passengers' appearance looked local, the most important changes couldn't be seen. Because of the harsh Prosperine environment, each individual's metabolism and respiratory system has also been modified. This allowed them to function in all ways as natives of the planet. Finally, their brown skin had been impregnated with a screening agent, without which the radiation from Prosperine's sun would kill them within a few days.

The ship pitched violently, and Gareth Blanquette muttered under his breath. He had been with Hickory and Jess on other assignments, and while he appreciated Jess's sense of fun, he didn't enjoy her cavalier approach to flying.

"Mother!" he burst out. "Why don't you just put the ship in control and let us cruise to the surface? You'll have everyone sick in a minute."

Here we go, thought Hickory. Gareth and Jess enjoyed a strange relationship. Jess was twice Gareth's age, and she had a tendency to treat him like her son. Gareth's response to this was to habitually refer to her as his 'mother.' They sparked off each other at every opportunity, but in any tight spot each would defend the other as if their own life depended on it.

"Quiet, boyo! Remember, you're the reason we're here. Sit back and relax, why don't you? You're making everyone nervous."

Gareth spluttered, "*I'm* making them nervous? You can't be serious."

"All right, that's enough," said Hickory, shaking her head. If she let them, they'd both carry on this way until they either landed or they crashed. "Jess?" She raised an eyebrow at her best friend.

"For heaven's sake, can't a girl have some fun?" said Jess. "Oh, alright." She snapped a switch on the dash; the craft sailed into the lower atmosphere and evened off.

They cruised until Hickory pointed to a flat, grassy area and Jess landed the ship without a shudder. She turned towards Gareth with a smirk on her face. "That's what you call flying, boyo." She tapped at a few keys and flicked a switch, and the engine whined into silence.

Looking at it on the viewscreen, the clearing had a ghostly feel to it. Tendrils of swirling vapor rose from the ground and disappeared into the hot air. In the mid-distance, a mist-shrouded thicket of stunted trees huddled together—the periphery of the jungle. Hickory signaled to Pat MacArthur, the engineer. "Paddy, bring your gear and the map. Let's see whereabouts we are."

The landing area measured roughly three hundred yards in diameter. When they exited the ship, the ground felt spongy underfoot, and a cloud of tiny flies erupted from the mist at every step. A fifty-foot high flat-topped pillar of rock stood to one side of the clearing. Hickory and the engineer climbed to the top and spread out the map.

MacArthur's chest heaved. "I hope the radiation protection they gave us works. It's hot as Hades out here."

"If it doesn't, we'll be dead in a couple of days, maybe less. So we better get on with it, eh?" Hickory laughed at the engineer's shocked expression and slapped him on the shoulder. "Don't worry, Paddy. This is my third visit to Prosperine, and I haven't had a problem yet. Our medical people are the best. Let's see what you've got."

"I wish we had some decent scanning equipment," said Paddy, smoothing his map on the rock surface. "They put this sketch together from orbit sightings. It's okay for distances and topography, but it won't help much with soil conditions like swamps, or sinkholes, or the biology around here."

Hickory shrugged. "Blame the admiral. He doesn't want to jeopardize his business relationship with the High Reeve by breaking the embargo on bringing advanced technology to the planet."

"I know there's a lot at stake, but I didn't realize the Scarf was part of Avanaux's jurisdiction," said Paddy.

"It is, according to Yonni. Which is why we have to rely on swords and knives for protection. We don't want to chance losing a blaster that might be picked up later by an inquisitive native. It's not as bad as it sounds. We can make do with what we have for now."

She studied the map and looked to the horizon through her spyglass. They'd landed on the edge of a shallow sea covered by several feet of tangled vines and seaweed that extended into the jungle. Beyond the trees, she could see a sparkle of light reflecting off more seawater. Further on, a large hill or perhaps a small mountain dominated the landscape. She checked her map. It was marked as one of many islands in the area. The entire area known as the Scarf was a network of thousands of islands connected by matted weed. Six hundred miles wide, it encircled the entire planet. "According to Brox, the jet should be just the other side of that jungle." She pointed. "Let's round up the others and get started."

*

"I can think of more pleasant places to take a stroll," said Gareth, readjusting his rucksack and squashing an insect against his cheek.

The two IA Rangers, Barb and Jack, grinned at each other as they led the way through the dense thicket. It was shadowy and oppressive beneath the intertwining branches. The air smelled fetid and was filled with the hum of tiny flies that sought out any uncovered part of the body. Often, one or other of the company tripped over tangled roots that seemed to spring up as they passed.

Hickory and Paddy followed next with Jess and Gareth bringing up the rear. *God, I hate jungle, but swampy jungle is worse,* thought Hickory. She swung her sword ferociously at a vine. The top half of the plant writhed away, spurting a viscous green fluid across Hickory's jacket. "Ughh. What the hell is that?" As she opened her mouth, a fly hit the back of her throat. She spluttered and coughed, then called a halt. She removed her jacket and scrubbed most of the sticky fluid off, but the jacket still smelled foul.

She tied a bandanna around her face, but this seemed to make things worse, with more and more flies attracted by the smell now pestering her eyes and ears. "This will drive me mad if we don't get away from here real quick," she shouted.

"We should reach the island in a few hours," said MacArthur, checking his map. "Hopefully, there'll be fewer flies when we get out of the trees." He called to the Rangers, "Jack, Barb, pick up the pace. We don't want to be stuck in this jungle when night falls."

Jess shivered. "Can't imagine anything worse," she muttered.

They shouldered their packs and stepped up their work rate. Hours of tramping through calf-deep mud took its toll, and before long, their boots and clothing were sodden and their feathered hair clung limply to their skulls.

When they found a dry patch, Hickory decided on a break and they stripped off their shoes and stockings. The constant damp had caused their skin to whiten and peel, and Gareth discovered that one of his feet was infested with a parasite. Barb, who doubled as a medic, cleaned and medicated the raw flesh, bandaged each toe separately and swaddled the entire foot in surgical tape.

"All right?" asked Jess, searching Gareth's face.

"Yeah. Picked up a couple of suckers, those tiny

bio-leeches, along the trail, but I think Barb got them all. Nasty little beggars."

"They're not the only nasties to worry about in here." She offered him a small olive-green block. "This is the last of the repellent Mack and I found on our first trip. Rub it over your face and arms," she said.

He took the block, weighed it in his hand, then gave it back. "Thanks, but I'll manage. You should keep it for yourself, or Hickory could do with it. The insects are tormenting the hell out of her."

Jess's eyes crinkled. "I just gave her the second last piece, you dope. Take it!" She laughed at his expression.

Hickory caught up with MacArthur. "How far to go, Paddy?" she asked.

The engineer checked his compass heading and peered at his map. He took a handkerchief from his pocket and wiped his forehead. "Tell the truth," he said eventually, "I'm not sure. There's nothing here to take a bearing from, but I'm pretty confident we're still headed roughly in the same direction as when we started. It seems to be becoming less dense, so I figure it can't be far. I'll send my two off on a recce, just in case we've strayed."

"Okay," said Hickory. "Gareth and Jess could do with some rest. We'll stay here until the Rangers return. Tell them no more than fifteen minutes out and fifteen back. The last thing I need is to have to go looking for them."

"Right," grunted MacArthur. He called his crew.

They waited for the scouts to return, resting their backs against a tree trunk.

"That insect repellent is ten times better than the stuff we were issued with, Jess, but it doesn't keep everything away." Hickory flicked a large furry orange and blue fly from her jacket.

"Not surprising, given how much your jacket stinks," said Gareth, screwing up his nose.

Hickory sighed. *I'm smelly, covered in insect bites, and I have the beginnings of an infection in my eye.* She rubbed at it with the back of her hand. *God, I could do with a bath.*

Five minutes before the Rangers were due back, a terrified cry forced them to their feet.

"That's Jack!" shouted MacArthur.

Hickory turned to Gareth, who was pulling on his boots. "You wait for Barb. I don't want her here on her own, thinking she's been left behind, soldier or not. She'd have heard that scream, too."

Gareth protested, but Hickory glared at him. "Gareth, just for once…" She turned and dashed into the bush, followed by Jess and the lumbering MacArthur. Jack had marked branches and left footprints to find his way back, so he was easy to follow. After about a quarter mile, Hickory paused.

The tell-tale signs ended at a well-trodden track leading left and right.

"Animal trail," said Jess. "I hope he didn't follow it."

They searched the ground on the both sides of the track but found no signs of the missing man.

"Damn!" said Hickory. "Which way?" They listened for any sounds from the engineer's aide.

Hickory probed in both directions using her empathic abilities, but could sense nothing. She was about to order them to split up when she heard a howl coming from the right-hand path.

Jess crouched and peered after the noise. "Sounds big, bigger than Jack," she whispered.

"And it's headed this way. Look out!" Hickory drew her sword and at the same time grabbed MacArthur by the arm, heaving him off the path. A short, muscular figure on two legs flashed past her. It was a blur of white fur, splattered with dark red blood.

Jess had only a fleeting glimpse of the fleeing creature before it disappeared into the forest. "What *was* that?" she asked.

"Not the small life-form the admiral told us to expect, that's for certain," said Hickory, wiping the blood from her blade. "We can talk about it later. We need to find Jack." She had a bad feeling they were already too late. Her empathic ability should have told her if he was nearby and in pain. She pulled MacArthur to his feet. "You okay, Paddy?"

The giant engineer brushed himself down, looking anxiously around him. "Has it gone? He was a big bloke. Knocked me off my feet like a skittle in the bowling alley."

Hickory winced and said, "I'm afraid that was mostly my fault. Sorry. Let's find Jack. He can't be far away."

A few minutes later, they found Paddy's assistant lying face down in the swamp. They turned him over, but he had stopped breathing. Jack's eyes were open, and three deep diagonal cuts ran across his face, chest and shoulder.

MacArthur turned from the sight and retched. "My God, that...that beast did this? Poor Jack. He was one of the good guys—he didn't deserve to die this way." His eyes widened in horror. "What am I going to tell his family?"

Five: Into the Swamp

Two hours later, they emerged from the jungle with Paddy and Jess carrying Jack's body on a makeshift stretcher. For the last half mile, the ground underfoot had become progressively softer and more marsh-like. Prosperine's two moons had dispersed the aurora, the smaller nestling on the surface of the sea and the other peeking above a twin-peaked mountain on the other side of a wide inlet.

A reed-filled quagmire stretched out for miles before them. Hickory searched left and right with her spyglass. "There's something about a mile over there." She pointed further up the edge of the jungle. "Hard to make out, but it could be our jet."

As they made their way across the marsh, bubbles of noxious gas burst on the brackish water all around them.

"Ugh," said Jess. This place stinks like something very unpleasant has died here."

"And the flies are worse than in the jungle." Barb swatted frantically at a group of multi-winged iridescent insects that buzzed around her face.

Hickory saw an orange blur scuttle away beneath the surface. "Keep to the matted weed and stay away from the water. The quicker we move, the sooner we'll get out of here," she said.

They set off at a trot, keeping close to the trees, with Paddy bringing up the rear. He waved them on when he saw them slow down to wait for him.

They closed in on the crashed spaceship. It rested on one side at the end of a deep hundred-yard-long furrow running parallel to the forest's edge. One of the short stabilizing wings had snapped off in the landing and lay half-buried in the weed forty feet further on from the fuselage. The signature swallow-tail of the Bikashi flyer towered high above them. Various smaller pieces of the ship's silvered hull and plastisteel windscreen were scattered around the crash site. The forward entry, just behind the cockpit, gaped empty like a missing tooth.

Hickory raised her arm. "The light is good, so I want a thorough search of the area before we get to the jet. The ground looks pretty treacherous, so be careful. Spread out between here and the trees. A hundred paces between us. Barb, you and Gareth stay on the far side and stick together. Jess, you're in the middle. Call out if you come across anything significant. I'll cover the area towards the sea."

Half an hour later the all met at the ship.

"Anything?" Hickory asked Jess.

"Looks like they were trying to make some running repairs." Jess showed them a hammer and some metal rods that were flat and blackened at the ends. "There's a makeshift forge." She nodded in the direction of the mound. "Also, this." She handed a blaster to Hickory.

Hickory examined the gun. "Empty." She passed it on to Gareth.

He looked at the weapon and frowned. "I swear this is the same gun Vogel pointed at me."

Hickory blinked. "One Bikashi blaster looks pretty much like another, I'd have thought." She inspected the metal rods then glanced back at the spacecraft. "Seems like a pretty hopeless task given the extent of the damage."

Gareth's brow wrinkled. "Whatever they were up to, they were disturbed. The trees over there are decorated with blood and shredded flesh. It's a pretty gruesome sight. From what I could tell there were three or four of them."

"Plus one between here and the jungle," said Barb. "His head's been ripped clean off his shoulders. Bikashi, but showing signs of massive radiation damage."

"Any idea how long he's been dead?" asked Hickory.

Barb glanced at Gareth, who nodded for her to

continue. "The burns were pre-death of course. A few flies and crawlers have found homes in the skulls, but they only moved in fairly recently. I'd say three, perhaps four days at most."

Jess nodded. "The fire looks relatively recent, too. I'd agree four days."

"So, five or six of them—a complete Bikashi squadron wiped out," said Hickory, "and they'd been here a fair while. This place looks lived in," said Hickory.

"Shock troops, eh? What could do this to a crack outfit like the Bikashi?" said Gareth.

Hickory clenched her jaw. "I think I can guess the answer to that. We saw in Erlach what the Riv-Amok is capable of. Let's take a look inside the ship."

The interior seemed in surprisingly good condition given the damage to the hull, thought Hickory. The lights were still operational, as was the Bikashi equivalent of washrooms, a meat freezer, and the ship's galley.

Jess returned from looking over the flight console in the cockpit. "Not even a glimmer of life from the engines. Someone's been trying to fix the radio, but with no luck."

Hickory eyed the shower. "We'll sleep in the jet tonight. I'll call the admiral and give him a progress report, then we'll give Jack a decent burial. But first…"

*

"Definitely Bikashi," said Hickory. She'd showered and washed her clothes, leaving them to dry on the ship's fuselage. Wearing Barb's ranger jacket, she felt infinitely better. She moved away from the ship, mostly to have some privacy on her call to the admiral, but also so that she could provide a good view of the ship via the voice activated transmitter in her hand. She noted that Gareth had followed her out. "There's the remains of a half dozen or so commandos scattered around the place. From the look of what's left, I'd say they've been massacred by the Riv-Amok or one of his kind."

The admiral appeared on the small screen, grim-faced. "Is it Vogel's personal transport? It was a gift from the Bikashi high command. There would be some personal items belonging to him—a commendation, amongst other things."

Hickory glanced at Gareth, them back at her transmitter. "There's nothing inside to indicate that it's his, but that doesn't mean it isn't, of course. There's not much left of the Bikashi troops except mangled body armor. To be honest, it looks as though they've been ripped apart, and their corpses most likely were eaten."

Gareth burst out before the admiral could reply. "No way! Uh, sorry admiral." He looked sheepishly at Hickory. "Sorry, Commander, but I just don't believe it. That bastard is far too cunning to be killed by an animal, no matter how big it is. He's here somewhere." He glanced around as though he might spot the Bikashi commander lurking in the undergrowth.

"Get a grip, Gareth," said Hickory, narrowing her eyes. "You go back to the ship, get some rest. I'll take it from here."

She watched as Gareth shuffled away, his hands deep in his pockets, then spoke quietly. "Sir, there are signs that at least one Bikashi survived the attack. We found an empty blaster and a campfire, a few days old. Also, there were footprints from the ship to the water. I believe he may have headed for El Toro Island."

"Maybe Gareth is right about it being Vogel."

"Sir, Gareth went through hell with Vogel and his scientists. It's natural his emotions run high where he's concerned, but I'd back his intuition. I certainly don't feel comfortable assuming Vogel's dead."

The admiral's eyebrows knitted together. "I'm not going to assume anything of the kind, commander. I'd love to get hold of that bastard. I'd be happy to send a squad of greenjackets to look for Vogel, but chances are they'd warn him off. And that's the last thing I want."

Hickory wondered whether sending in the greenjackets wasn't the best option. After all, they were the Agency's elite marines and specialists at operating behind enemy lines without being caught. But Gareth and the admiral were right. This Bikashi had a knack for getting out of tight spots. And if he remained on the loose, he could become a significant threat, especially if he got his hands on the sword.

She thought about asking the admiral to drop a dinghy to make the crossing quicker, but realized he wouldn't risk spooking Vogel. "I'll call you when we get to the island, sir."

Six: Something in the Water

They gave Jack a sea burial and watched as his body floated away, buoyed up by some reeds. Paddy said a few words, mostly about Jack's service record and his fondness for practical jokes. Jack wasn't religious, he said, but he thought the ranger wouldn't mind a silent prayer to mark his passing, and they bowed their heads self-consciously. The cadaver made it a few hundred yards off shore before there was a disturbance in the water and it disappeared.

"Better than being buried in the ground around here," said Paddy.

They stayed by the water's edge watching the moonlight illuminate El Toro's twin peaks. The island looked tantalizingly close, separated from them by this narrow stretch of sea. Iridescent froth sparkled on the tops of small waves that extended as far as Hickory could see on either side. "Can everyone swim?" she asked.

"It doesn't look that bad—maybe a mile," said

Gareth, looking through the spyglass.

"I haven't been swimming for a long time," said Barb, "but I did a mile at basic training."

"Swim like a fish," said Paddy. He smacked his oversized chest. "Or a whale more like. Anyway, the distance won't bother me."

Jess looked doubtfully towards the mountain, then sighed. "I don't suppose we've much choice, do we?"

Hickory shook her head. "I know we're all tired, but we have to get to the island as quickly as we can. So here's the plan. We don't have the tools to make a raft big enough to carry us all, and even if we did it would take us days to build. Instead, we make a small one to float our backpacks on and push it in front of us. We can get that done in a couple of hours, then we eat and rest up until the morning. Hopefully, the crossing will look easier in daylight."

"Who needs sleep?" said Gareth. "We've only been on the go for fourteen hours."

Jess and Barb searched for wood along the edge of the forest, and Gareth and Hickory trimmed and tied the pieces together with vines to form a makeshift raft. When they finished, Hickory looked at it critically. "It should do the trick. The water is flat, and there's not that much of a current." They retreated to the Bikashi jet, ate sparingly from their rations then huddled together in their weather packs.

Jess heard Barb sniffling softly and put an arm around her. "Don't cry, little one. Things will look brighter in the morning. You'll see."

"I can't stop thinking about Jack. What a terrible way to die."

"Were you close to him?" said Jess.

"He was a nice guy, but no…we weren't close— not in that way. It's just…that monster! It ripped him to shreds. What was it?"

Hickory spoke in the darkness. "I've been thinking about that myself. I'm glad we didn't bump into any others."

Gareth snapped his fingers. "That could be it, you know. It's feasible this is a solitary animal— probably a male—and Jack could have unwittingly trespassed on its territory. The beast probably felt it needed to defend itself when it saw another large bipedal male."

Hickory felt unsure about Gareth's explanation. In the second it fled past her, she'd seen that the beast was wounded, possibly by a sword. It had been in agony, and angry, and might have associated Jack with its pain. She guessed its attacker was one of the Bikashi. But she agreed with Gareth to help put Barb's mind at rest. "I think it's a jungle creature, so we shouldn't meet any more of them—not out here anyway."

*

Hickory woke early but lay until the first rays of daybreak pushed the darkness back. She made a hot infusion of herbs that refreshed her more than her sleep and then, as Prosperine's bright orange sun came over the horizon, she woke the others.

The raft looked less sturdy than it had appeared in the moonlight, and they spent part of the morning strapping another layer of driftwood on top before they dragged it to the water's edge and launched it. They stripped off their clothes and boots and stowed them in their packs, then loaded up the raft and set off. The water shelved quickly. Almost immediately, they found themselves out of their depth. They swam, pushing the raft in front of them. It proved to be seaworthy and floated high on the surface, but the current felt stronger than Hickory had anticipated, and it tugged them along the channel towards the open sea.

"Swim with the current but at an angle to the island," shouted Hickory. "We're caught in a rip, and we need to conserve our energy. We should get free of it after a couple of hundred feet."

The rip was wider than Hickory had thought and after forty minutes with no relief in sight, she became worried. They had been driven almost level with the tip of the island, and a stiff breeze had sprung up, creating an uncomfortable swell. Barb looked just about spent. *I hope there aren't any sharks on*

Prosperine. Beneath the waves, she could see shadowy forms of large and small marine life swimming over the seabed below. There didn't seem to be any sharks.

Barb screamed when the water erupted a few yards in front of them. A long, slender shape launched into the air, writhing upwards, water streaming from its fluorescent skin. Two butterfly-shaped, translucent fins unfolded from just behind an elongated bottom jaw and propelled the fish fifty feet into the air. The creature's mouth opened, revealing jagged saw-teeth that snapped around an unsuspecting seabird flying overhead. The creature folded its fins and fell back, creating hardly a ripple as it disappeared below the surface.

"Jesus," swore Gareth. "What was that?" His eyes darted around, fearfully.

The strength returned to Hickory's legs, and she kicked furiously. "Get paddling. Whatever it is, I doubt its diet is restricted to birds."

"It didn't have any eyes," said Jess, grunting from her renewed effort. "How did it know the bird was there?"

"Must have some other method of sensing the environment. Maybe sonic or infrared," said Gareth.

"Gareth! For God's sake just swim!" Jess gritted her teeth and forced her legs to move faster.

Finally, they escaped the current and steered the

raft directly towards the island, but progress was difficult in the rolling waves. Three hundred yards from shore, Barb's knuckles had turned white from gripping the raft, and her legs trailed behind her, barely moving. Her breathing came in bursts, and she swallowed gulps of water. She called out in a shrill voice. "Pat, I can't hang on. Arms too tired, hands feel numb."

Hickory felt pricks in her legs like pins and needles and shouted to the others, "Keep moving! There're lice in the water."

At that moment, the raft lurched, propelled upward by a breaking wave. Barb's hands were torn free. She kicked feebly to regain her hold, but the current quickly dragged her away.

Paddy and Gareth took off after her, with Gareth quickly making up the distance. Barb spluttered and flapped in the water, her eyes wide with fear. "Easy, Barb," he said. "I've got you, I won't let go." He swam behind the panicking ranger and cupped her chin in one hand. "Come on, kick, you can make it."

A flurry in the water fifty yards away caught Hickory's eye A school of small gold and silver fish were leaping in and out of the water, heading in Gareth's and Barb's direction. "I don't like the look of that," she groaned.

Jess shouted at Gareth to re-double his efforts. "Get a move on, boyo—there's something in the water!"

Hickory searched for the engineer and saw him swimming lazily back to the raft. She lost sight of him in the choppy water, then thought she heard him shout.

Ten minutes later, Gareth's feet touched the bottom, and he helped Barb struggle through the fast shoaling water. A few of the tiny fish followed them into the shallows and lunged at Barb. Gareth smacked them away with his hand as they nipped at her thighs and calves.

Hickory and Jess raced up the beach and hauled Barb onto the safety of the sand.

"Where's Paddy?" asked Gareth, looking around for the genial engineer.

Hickory shook her head at Gareth and pulled Barb into a hug. She whispered. "I'm sorry, Barb. Paddy didn't come back. He almost made it to the raft, but the fish got him. He didn't stand a chance, poor guy." She hesitated, frowning over Barb's shoulder at the others. "They attacked like piranhas."

"Noooo! It should have been me," said Barb, pulling away and sobbing. "First Jack, and now Pat." She faltered. "He tried to save me and ended up dead. I wasn't strong enough, it should have been me." She fell to her knees and bent over, burying her face in her hands.

Jess reached out to her, kneeling by her side and wrapping her arms around her. "You can't blame yourself for that. He and Jack were good men. Paddy tried to do the right thing, which was his nature. Everyone knew the risks of a trip like this. There's always danger. We're all part of the same team, and we'd all do the same thing if it came to it. Nobody knew anything about those piranha fish before we got here. It's just bad luck." She held Barb by the shoulders and smiled at her.

The girl sniffled, and Hickory covered her shoulders with a long cloth and rubbed her arms.

"I guess so," Barb said slowly. "Gareth, I'm sorry, I didn't thank you for saving my life." She looked up at him, the tears streaming down her cheeks.

Gareth face turned red, and he shrugged. "That's okay. I'm really sorry about Paddy."

Hickory let out a long shuddering breath and looked around. *Less than twenty-four hours into this mission and already I've lost two of the team.* She set her jaw and gathered herself together. She was the group leader, and they still had a job to do. "Let's get our stuff off the raft and get dressed. It's time for us to go. We need to get higher up the mountain before we set up camp. No knowing what we might meet up with when the sun goes down."

They scrambled up the rocky hillside for most of the afternoon and into the early evening. It felt cooler here, and the sky was streaked with ribbons of green, blue and orange from the ionic curtain that surrounded Prosperine. When they reached a plateau, Hickory stopped and looked around. "This looks as good a place as any. There's a stream over there, and plenty of wood for a fire. Let's get set up."

Hickory debated whether to set a sentry. They were all exhausted, but her training kicked in. "Two hours guard duty," she said. "I'll take the first shift. You take the next one, Jess, then you, Gareth. Barb…" She paused. The ranger was already snug in her weather pack, fast asleep.

*

Next morning, Gareth woke Jess. "I think I'll take a quick look around before breakfast. I heard a couple of violators howling an hour ago. We don't want any surprises today," he said.

"Be careful," said Jess. "And don't be long."

"I'm always careful, mother. Make mine black with two." He grinned at Jess's scowl, strapped on his sword, and set off.

Twenty minutes later Gareth hurried back into the camp, breathing rapidly, his face on fire. "Hickory, Jess, you're not going to believe this. There's someone camped down on the beach!"

Hickory rose slowly from the fire and wiped her hands on her trousers. Her heartbeat raced. "What kind of camp? Where?"

"There's a lagoon about five miles away, on the other side of the island from where we came ashore. It's just a lean-to, made from driftwood. You can see it from the top of that ridge."

Hickory's eyes followed Gareth's pointing finger.

"That's not the only thing," he said looking straight at Jess, his head bobbing up and down. "It's Vogel. It has to be."

"No!" Jess shook her head, disbelievingly.

"Yes!"

Hickory held up her hand. "Wait, Gareth, did you see him? You can't be sure it's a Bikashi from that distance, never mind Vogel."

Gareth snorted. "Who else on Prosperine could survive a crash in a spaceship, an attack by the Riv-Amok, and the sharks and piranhas in the sea?" He saw Barb blanch and felt immediately contrite. "Sorry, Barb. I didn't mean to…"

"Did you see him?" Hickory repeated her question. The Bikashi commander was the most fearsome opponent she'd ever met. He'd been rescued by his own people after the battle for Ezekan city had been won by the government forces. Vogel might easily have killed Gareth and Jess right then, but he had chosen to spare them—a fact that still puzzled her. At the time they'd all assumed Vogel had hightailed it to his home planet of Auriga. She felt a sour taste in her mouth at the thought that the admiral might be right, and he might never have left Prosperine.

She glanced at the sky. It would be full light in less than half an hour. "Did you see any signs of life?" she asked again.

Gareth shook his head slowly. "Hard to tell from where I stood. He could be down there right now." He looked to both Jess and Barb, then Hickory. He blushed vividly as nobody spoke. "Okay, maybe it did look pretty deserted."

"We'll go after breakfast. There's no sense in risking a broken leg or worse in this half-light." As he opened his mouth to argue, Hickory said, "It can wait, Gareth."

Seven: A Meeting of Friends

Hickory spoke with the admiral from the beach. "It's an old shelter, sir. Likely from a shipwrecked mariner, but it's been occupied recently. There are boot prints all around, most leading to the jungle."

"Sounds like that's our alien. How long since he's been there, do you think?"

"Only a day or two. We're just setting up our search parameters, and we'll be in pursuit."

"Good. I'll place a security perimeter around the island, a mile off the beach. We'll know if he attempts to leave." The admiral paused. "I'm sorry to hear about Pat MacArthur. He was a good man— one of the best I've worked with. I had the honor of calling him, my friend."

"Yes, sir. He was a brave man, too. Will you be contacting his family?"

"It's part of the job, Hickory, a sad part. How is Barb coping?"

"Not the best. It's hit her pretty hard. First Jack,

then Paddy."

The admiral pursed his lips. "I've had an urgent call from the Agency, and I'll be gone a few days. Apparently, there's a problem at the space terminal on Dominion Island. I'll fly past this afternoon and take Barb with me. You should continue to search for the Sword of Connat-sèra-Haagar. It's even more important if the Bikashi is free and loose. Have you had any ideas about that?"

"I have, sir, but they're built on too many assumptions. I'd rather keep them to myself, at least until I get a little more evidence to support them."

"Very well, Commander. I'll see you this afternoon."

*

From the camouflaged hide at the edge of the woods, Vogel watched the landing craft skim over the waves and land on the beach. He'd arrived back from his reconnaissance of the island earlier that morning and almost walked into the Earth people sniffing around his shelter. He had been shocked to see them, but the conversation he heard between the witch and her superior proved enlightening. They were looking for the sword, and they'd found his jet and tracked him to here!

He let the goldengrass rebound slowly back to vertical and retreated into the woods. The young one had looked straight at him but hadn't seen him. He cursed his bad luck. Those three had given him a lot of trouble and the boy, especially, was like a hungry *tintarra* on the trail of its prey. He would never let up—one glimpse would be all he needed. He should have killed him after the battle for Ezekan when he had the chance, but he'd succumbed to a rare moment of pity. The boy had suffered much at the hands of his scientists, and he'd thought to spare him. And then the foolhardy youngster had taken the opportunity to throw his dagger at him! He snorted. He wouldn't be so generous the next time.

Vogel could feel the sword urging him to combat, but there were too many of them to be sure of victory. His proboscis twitched, and he eyed the landing craft greedily. The Bikashi needed to get back to Ezekan. The human had said he would fly the shuttle to the space station on Dominion Island and take a bubble-craft to the IA's orbital platform. Could he climb aboard undetected, hitch a ride, find his way to the mainland, maybe even discover a way off this forsaken planet? He felt something prod at his consciousness. *The sword belongs here.* He pushed the thought away. His first priority was to get off this island, to get away from the Scarf. He watched the humans trek across the sand towards the beach shelter.

*

The Bikashi trotted through the trees to the blind

side of the shuttle. He waited until he felt sure the craft was empty before he climbed inside. The human sleeping in the cargo hold took him by surprise, but it was the handler's bad luck that he had decided to grab a nap while the admiral and the others were away. Vogel approached silently, reached for his neck and broke it with a snap. He hauled the corpse into the back of the cargo bay and dumped it in a storage chest.

Fifteen minutes later, the admiral, his pilot, and a female boarded. The IA officer seemed agitated and in a hurry to get to his meeting. He didn't notice the absence of his crewman.

It took less than an hour for the shuttle to reach the spaceport at Dominion Island. The pilot parked on the site reserved for small ship arrivals, adjacent to the main terminal. Vogel knew from his interrogation of the Earth boy that the core contained the landing control, quarantine and planet-acclimatization facilities for the Agency. The space elevator that transported personnel to and from the orbiting space station was also here. Could he get to orbit and flag down a ship headed for a friendly star system? It seemed a forlorn hope. There would be communications equipment on the space station, but it was highly improbable that a friendly ship would happen to be in the vicinity at the right time.

When the Earthlings disappeared into the

terminal, Vogel crept from his hiding place. He was acutely aware of his alien form. He had managed to go unnoticed for a short time amongst the Avanauri with his features heavily disguised. His natural appearance would cause panic amongst the natives, who would most likely think him a demon. He considered stripping the dead crewman of his uniform, but that would be little better than what he already wore.

Vogel searched the ship's lockers and found a variety of formal and casual dress kept on board for the admiral's use. A long black robe lined with silver, knee-length boots and a wide brimmed hat was the best of the available choices. The clothes were of a style and quality that a wealthy merchant or politician might wear. Not ideal, but they would have to serve.

Hurriedly, he dressed and threw his old clothes in the chest, covering the dead man. He packed what food he could find and several bottles of water into his shoulder satchel, then cautiously exited the shuttle. He glanced about him, scurried across the clearing, and darted into the forest. Every second, he expected to hear the alarm being raised. He looked back from behind a tree, his heart pounding with excitement, but everything remained quiet.

To reach Avanaux, he had to get to the coast and find a boat. But which way? The spaceport had been built in the highlands, surrounded by dense forest. He crept through the trees encircling the buildings and found a pathway leading downhill. He set a fast pace, darting back into the trees when any stranger came in sight.

Vogel arrived in the early hours of the morning at a fishing village and crept stealthily to the waterfront. Three naurs were busy loading flying fish onto a boat. He crouched behind a cart and listened to their conversation.

A heavily muscled naur heaved a full basket onto the deck. "Be quick, Lach," he said. "The markets will open in a few hours. If we miss the start, the biggest buyers will be gone, and we'll have to make do with the small farmers."

The third of the trio snorted. "Don't listen to him, Lach. We have time. Jerrik is only worried that someone else will pay coin for his favorite nauri before he gets there."

Jerrik laughed. "Cherili is more pleasing to the eye than the whores in the fleshpots of Harbor Town where you two spend your money."

Vogel waited until the naurs were ready to set sail. Sliding silently aboard, he hid amongst the baskets of fish destined for the fields of Avanaux, to be used as fertilizer.

He slipped over the side in the pre-dawn light as the boat moored alongside a jetty in Harbor Town.

Pulling his collar up and his hat down, he made sure the sword could not be seen, then pushed his hands deep into his pockets and joined the bustling crowd of peddlers, sailors, shipwrights, merchants, fishermen and foreigners from all parts of the northern continent.

The Bikashi avoided the direct route to Ezekan, and instead hiked through the hills and orchards that surrounded the capital. He had come this way only once before, plotting rebellion with the Pharlaxian leader Sequana and the Earthman Nolanski. He breathed a sigh of relief when he reached his destination—the underground tunnel that led into the Temple of Balor was still passable.

Vogel rested at the end of the tunnel until he thought the last of the worshipers would have left. He finished off the remains of his store of food, then pushed with his shoulder against the door. It groaned open slowly, and he slipped through the gap. A curtain on the other side hid the entry from curious eyes, and he waited behind this until the temple was empty.

As he emerged, flickering flames from a great iron fire pit sent his shadow dancing across the carving of the four faces of Balor that formed one wall of the temple. A grotto dedicated to Connat-sèra-Haagar stood against one wall, halfway to the main entrance. Vogel stared at the heroine with her empty sword hand poised above the dead and dying enemy at her feet. He gripped the handle of the sword at his waist. There could be no doubt. This was the weapon that had been cut free of the stone. Quickly, he made his way to a side exit and squeezed through.

He needed to find a better disguise, one that would stand closer scrutiny in the city's public places. He searched amongst the poor districts for a store selling recycled clothing and found one in a dark laneway. He scaled the wall to the rear of the property and forced the door lock with the sword. It opened with a click.

Inside, he helped himself to some rags—a dull, threadbare cloak that stretched from his neck to his feet and a pair of boots that were less fashionable and a better fit than those he currently wore. He chose some long sleeved gloves to cover the scales on his hands and wrapped a dirty scarf around his face in the manner of one afflicted by the wasting disease, prevalent in the city. Finally, he pulled the hood of the cloak low over his head to shade his eyes.

Satisfied his appearance would excite little response other than to encourage others to avoid him, he left the store and walked unhurriedly to the edge of town.

He found the place he sought—a tavern frequented by Sequana's followers in the days before the war—and opened the door. The smell of cooking made his head swim. He would have preferred a haunch of bloody meat, but the aroma of new baked bread and roast vegetables seemed like ambrosia of the Gods. There were a number of Avanauri partaking of the evening meal. In a shadowy corner, he spied what he sought. A few disheveled individuals were hunched over a table, segregated from the rest of the patrons.

"What are you doing there?" A servant, holding a tray piled with food in one hand, stood ten feet away and stared at him belligerently. "*Haravashi* are not allowed to enter through the front door. Go to the hole quickly before you are seen."

Vogel grunted, then shuffled his way over to the area set aside for the unfortunates in every Avanauri hostel. He passed a table laden with scraps, day old corn bread and pots of steaming stews from yesterday's dinner. The waiter called after him.

"Don't you know anything? If you have a bowl, take some soup. If not, you'll have to be content with some corn bread and raw honey. Drop your two cerstes in the basin at the end and take a seat at the table with your friends."

Vogel picked up two pieces of bread, dipped them in the pot of honey and threw a couple of small coins he had taken from the clothing shop into the receptacle. The others at the table, a ramshackle foursome dressed in rags and sporting dirty bandages on several parts of their body, did no more than glance at him before they returned to their meal.

The Bikashi felt his stomach growl and wolfed down the bread. It barely took the edge off his hunger, but he didn't want to risk the ire of the waiter by going for more. One by one, the other *haravashi* finished their scraps and left. He knew it wouldn't be long before the waiter arrived to move him on, but he would stay as long as possible. He settled down to wait and tuned his ears to the conversation around him.

"...and the government should be ashamed of persecuting a naur like the Teacher..."

"...those *haravashi* shouldn't be allowed in the same room as decent folk..."

"...kill all the Erlachi, I say..."

"...told me it was some sort of giant flying beast..."

"...he was mad, I tell you. He would have killed us all..."

Vogel's eyes swiveled towards the source of this last comment. A tall, unkempt individual leaned against the bar speaking with the landlord. His speech sounded slurred, and he slopped the contents of his tankard onto the counter.

The naur had consumed too much of the potent Avanauri ale, and the bartender encouraged him to leave. "Tell me about it when you're sober, Thurle.

I can't understand a word you say when you've been drinking like this. Go home and go to bed."

With a stab of excitement, Vogel recognized the drunk as Sequana's lieutenant. Thurle—the one who had been a nephew of the Chief Peacekeeper. A treacherous piece of work, he thought. He had betrayed not only his uncle but the rest of his family when he joined the revolutionaries with Sequana.

Vogel felt surprise that the naur had survived the final battle. He had seen him riding beside Sequana when the cursed Charakai had attacked. Thurle would know where to find the rebel chieftain.

Sequana had welcomed the Bikashi to his cause, and the two had developed a grudging respect for each other. He was one of the few Avanauri citizens aware of the alien presence on Prosperine. He was also his best bet for getting off this planet, as he had contact with the various smuggler groups that might give him passage for a fee.

He saw the waiter making a bee-line for him and stood up slowly from the table.

"Don't forget. Backdoor. There behind you. Can't have you bumping into any of the clientele, can we?" He scowled as Vogel hobbled slowly towards the exit. "Hurry! And make sure you've got everything. I don't want you leaving behind a diseased rag or spoon."

*

The lieutenant swayed as he made his way across the common area between the inner and outer walls of Ezekan. This was the domain of the homeless and less fortunate naurs, the perpetually poor, the ex-criminals, the diseased and the freed prisoners from the revolution and their families. In contrast to the rest of the city, there were no large communes here, only wooden shacks and tents crowded against the walls on either side of an open sewer.

Ignoring the stench, Vogel confronted Thurle before he reached his destination.

Thurle yelped and leaped out of the way as Vogel reached towards him. "Go away you disgusting filth! What do you want? I have nothing for you." He crossed his hands under his armpits and hunched his shoulders to make himself a smaller target for the bandaged hand.

"Thurle, you know me," said the Bikashi in a guttural voice.

The lieutenant scowled. "I don't care who you are. I have no money. Let me be. I don't want your diseased carcass anywhere near me."

"Shrelek! I have no disease," roared Vogel, tearing the cloth from his face.

Thurle's mouth opened and shut several times before he could stutter, "Vogel…Vogel? Is it you?"

"How many other Bikashi are you acquainted with, naur?"

The Avanauri made to embrace the commander, then drew back, unable to meet Vogel's eyes. "I'm sorry. Please excuse my foolishness, commander. It's just that I haven't seen any of my old comrades for a long time." He choked and mumbled, "Most are dead, now."

"Comrade?" Vogel's laugh was a low growl that set his proboscis quivering. He studied the naur through hooded eyes. "Ah, so we were. We fought together against a common enemy."

"And for a common cause," said Thurle. "Come, we are almost at my home, primitive as it is. I have a bottle of Erlachi wine that I have stored for just such an occasion."

Vogel let the reference pass. The Avanauri seemed in a bad way. His face looked pale and sickly, and he had a pathetically hopeful light in his eyes. His jacket was soiled and tattered at the sleeves, and his shoulders were hunched as though he carried a great burden. Clearly, the peace had not been kind to him.

Thurle jumped across a trickle of sewage and beckoned the Bikashi to follow. The naur pulled aside a canvas flap covering the entry to his cabin and ushered Vogel inside. "The locals looted and set fire to this place when I first arrived. I managed to save everything except a few baubles and the door." He grinned as though this were a great joke. "Come in, sit at the table. I will fetch the bottle. Where have you been all this time? What is it—six months since we lost the battle at Ezekan?"

The Bikashi did not respond.

"Where did I put the goblets? Ah, here they are." Thurle wiped the ornate cups with a rag and poured some of the dull red liquor into each. "It's not been easy around here, I can tell you," he said, placing one cup before Vogel. He sat opposite and raised his wine in a toast then drained half of it. "Still, what can you expect?" He fiddled with the stem of the goblet. "We might have been as oppressive in victory, had Balor smiled on us." He glanced at Vogel's cup, which lay untouched. "Not drinking? It's a good brew, I assure you."

Vogel stared unblinkingly at Thurle. His eyes and mouth were narrow slits and his nose for once was still. "I am not interested in your wine."

The voice growled low and threatening, and Thurle shrank back in his chair. "What do you want with me?" In his agitation, he knocked over his goblet.

"I want to find Sequana. Where is he?"

Thurle's shoulders relaxed. He wiped an arm across his forehead, then refilled his cup. "Balor, Vogel! I thought you were going to kill me." He let out a long shuddering laugh, then fell silent. After a few moments, he continued, "Sequana is dead, murdered by the Castalienan whore. He tried to rally the Erlachi to his cause, but they resisted his charms, compelling though they were. Sequana, himself, fell under the spell of the Sword of Connat-sèra-Haagar, Balor curse it. It drove him to madness. He trusted no one, not even me. In the end, he took to murdering his own—even his loyal nauris bodyguard."

Sequana is dead? Vogel controlled himself with an effort. "How did he come by the Sword?"

"He ordered me to take it from the Temple of Balor. It felt wrong to me, but Sequana insisted on it. I don't know what happened to it after his death." He glanced uneasily at the weapon that the Bikashi wore at his side.

Vogel took the blade from its makeshift scabbard and slapped it on the table between them. "This is the sword?" He already knew the answer, but needed Thurle to be sure of it in his own mind.

"That is the Sword of Connat-sèra-Haagar that I took from the temple and gave to Sequana. How come you by it?" He cringed away from the table.

"It is mine by right of conquest, kinslayer."

Thurle's eyes opened wide, and he half rose, his hand reaching for the dagger at his side. "What say you? Have you been driven mad, too?"

The Bikashi commander laughed. "You are not the first to think so. No, it is whispered in the taverns of Ezekan that Josipe-sèr-Amagon died in the dungeons of Kandromena cursing your name."

"How do you…? I…I did not mean for him to die. I would have released him, but…" He trailed off in the force of Vogel's gaze, then his fury returned. "He did nothing for me. I was family, but he kept me in the ranks, never showed me care or respect. I'm glad he died!"

"Of course. I do not condemn you for it. Any Bikashi soldier would do the same." He paused and searched the Avanauri's eyes for long moments. Eventually, he said, "Thurle, the sword is mine to command, and you know something of the strength it gives to he who wields it." He waited until the naur nodded, then continued, "We are embarking on a great journey, this sword and I, one that will deliver great riches at its end. I need to engage the services of half a dozen worthy fighters. Will you join me as my lieutenant and submit to my authority?"

Thurle's mouth gaped like a fish and his eyes widened. "Wha… what kind of riches?"

Vogel waved a hand carelessly. "Let us say there will be enough treasure for you to live out the rest of your life in splendor and allow you to indulge in every sumptuous delight your mind can imagine." He smiled. The battle being fought among his emotions played out clearly on the naur's face. Poverty and the desperate need to be thought worthy struggled against his fear of the Bikashi and the sword.

"Where will the journey take us? Where is this treasure to be found?" Thurle licked his lips, hope gleaming in his eyes.

"We must go to the Scarf."

Thurle's chest deflated, and his head dropped to his chest. "We must go to our death to be rich? That is no bargain."

"It will be a long and arduous journey, and some may die, yes, but we will have food and drink to comfort us along the way. With a little luck and a lot of courage, we may survive to enjoy our wealth. Thurle, I have been there, and I have returned. It will be easier with companions."

The Avanauri gazed around his home. A cold draft whistled through the gaps in the walls. He had chopped up the door for firewood, but none remained. A bed of straw lay against the far wall, home to a family of rats and an army of fleas. There was nothing to put in the pot—if there were a pot to put it in, that is. The sum total of his wealth was in this room: two chairs, a table, and two battered goblets.

*

It wasn't the best solution, thought Vogel. He would have preferred to deal with Sequana, who could have arranged a meeting with the Dark Suns to get him off this planet. He would have returned later with a troop of Bikashi Warriors to claim the prize he had left on the island. But with Sequana dead, he could see no better way to escape. The alternative had been a spur of the moment decision. Convincing the Avanauri had been simple. The naur was desperate for a change in fortune and would do anything, go anywhere, to achieve it.

Vogel still didn't know how he would get off the planet, not in detail, but he'd improvise once he had a better handle on the situation. Anything was better than hanging around this city until he was caught.

Thurle had left for Harbor Town to recruit the six fighters he needed. Vogel had warned him not to reveal his identity, and to hire only villains who were highly skilled in the use of sword and bow. He would personally assess their skills before they set sail. Thurle had already chartered a fast ship for the voyage. Its master was a black-hearted murderer who drove his crew like slaves and would sell his mother, if he had one, for a small pile of the devil's coin.

All being well, the journey should take three or four days. Thurle would be his lieutenant, his voice to the crew. He, himself, would stay below until they were well under way, only coming on deck at night. He planned to take on extra supplies at Dominion Island, then head to the twin-peaked island in the Scarf via the Karack Channel. He closed his eyes. If he could find it. The Karack Channel belonged almost to the realms of myths and legends. It was reputed to be the sole sea passage between Avanaux and Castaliena, the great northern and southern continents of Prosperine. The captain claimed that over the years, a few mariners had navigated through the Scarf to get to Avanaux and vice versa, but the charts, such as they were, had been shown to be unreliable.

The sword had whispered to him to return to the Scarf, that it would show him the way. He hoped his faith in it was not misplaced. He also hoped he wasn't losing his mind.

Eight: Visions

Connat-sèra-Haagar sat hunched on the wooden throne, her hands and forehead resting on the pommel of the sword. It had been many years since the war with the Erlachi, an eon it seemed since she first held the sword aloft. Her strength had been unequaled in all of Avanaux, and she had slept little, filling her nights with an insatiable appetite for learning.

Now, staying awake had become a challenge, and she could not remember the last book she'd read. The pigmentation around her neck and cheekbones had turned dark brown, and the strip of feathery hair that grew from her brow to her shoulders was limp and dull. The skin covering her still-muscular frame was translucent leather. She raised empty eyes to the sky, seeking divine inspiration.

The bond between she and the sword had grown stronger with each passing year. In the beginning, she'd resisted the cravings for power, but slowly, insidiously, the sword had asserted its grip until it seemed she had no will other than that of the sword. Together, they had become a fierce and indomitable force, forging the warlike and politically disparate territories of Avanaux into a powerful, united nation.

She thought she'd become a fair, a wise, ruler since defeating the Erlachi. She'd put in place a system for representative government and introduced many improvements to better the lives of her people. But, as her pigmentation changed from the beautiful green and purple of her youth to this dark mockery of the flowering she had never experienced, it seemed that the opportunity, even her desire for battle, had waned. She had become old. And then the sword began to whisper its secrets of strange places and stranger beings. In these final days, she had come to know the real purpose of the sword and she wept.

She called for parchment and writing implements and wrote:

The sword that some call the Sword of Connat and others call the Sword of Balor was forged long before the birth of the Avanauri, the Erlachi or any other people of Avanaux, save the Lonilki. The father of life breathed the gift of invisibility into his servants, the Lonilki, so that they might escape the ravages of time and continue to pay him homage. You know them. The Lonilki live by the gates of Balor's palace and have dwelt there longer even than the

Masters of the Sword.

The sword was not created by Balor, but the all-seeing Balor permitted it to be forged in the great fires of the Segniori, a peaceful people, in their time of need. In that year, the Segniori saw the world was ending. The days were long and dry, and the sun rose in the sky with a terrible light and heat that oppressed the people. Crops shriveled in the fields, and the yarrak died of thirst in great numbers. Balor led the leaders of the Segniori to a new country in a land far from the sun, and he instructed them to build two great chariots to carry all the people and their treasure to their new home.

Before the Segniori could complete their task, they were challenged by a savage warrior race from the sky who threatened to destroy the Segniori and all their works. The learned ones of the Segniori made a plan and forged the sword, granting it great power, so that it would forever protect the peoples of Prosperine from danger.

A thousand years passed before the Wargus returned, but they were vanquished by Saarg the Destroyer, and fled, vowing to come again.

The purpose of the sword is to defend all the inhabitants of Prosperine from destruction. It was not created for battle between Avanauri and Erlachi, neither by any naur against any other. The penalty for such is madness and death. I, Connat-sèra-

Haagar, greatest warrior of the Avanauri, tell you this with my dying breath. The sword must be guarded in the Temple for all time until it awakens to protect all the peoples of Prosperine.

Connat-sèra-Haagar signed the document and laid down the pen. She had written a true account of what the sword had told her, but it was not the entire truth. She hoped it would be enough.

*

The Shrine of Honor was a modest building, built to honor the victories of Connat-sèra-Haagar over the Erlachi more than a thousand years previously. It was tucked away in a small park just north of the Smith precinct. Unlike the majority of gardens in Ezekan that grew vegetable crops, it was filled with decorative flowering plants. The Teacher, Kar-sèr-Sephiryth often came here with his disciples to pray. He could pass an hour without being pressed by supplicants or priests.

As he lay prostrate at the feet of the effigy of Balor, perspiration dripped from his forehead onto the rose-colored steps, turning them a deep red.

His closest followers observed his agony and glanced at each other in distress. They did not comprehend the suffering of their leader during those moments, neither could they share in nor help relieve it.

Kar cried aloud in anguish as though a beloved

child had been taken from him by a deadly illness. "Balor, your will is mine. If I must endure torment that your people may live, then let it be so. Strengthen my resolve with your love and compassion until your spirit is taken from me. Guide my actions and provide me with the wisdom to achieve your purpose and lead your people to your truth."

He remained kneeling, his face bathed in radiance, then rose to his feet and went into the garden.

The Teacher walked aimlessly amongst the bushes and flowers. He thought on the message of the two visions he had received. His dream of the last days of Connat-sèra-Haagar had shed light on the sword. Since he first beheld it, he had known it was more than mere metal. He had asked the Riv-Amok to take it to the Scarf because he sensed it posed a terrible danger. The dream had shown him that the sword had a vital purpose, but needed to be held by an earnest hand. Connat's last command confirmed this.

The meaning of the second vision was less clear but more terrifying. He would endure a trial of his faith and Balor would turn his face from him. He shivered at the glimpse Balor had given him of this future. It was an emptiness beyond imagination, a devastation of everything he held close.

Balor had whispered that he must be one with the sword, must go to the Scarf when the hour of need arose. He prayed that he would not fail his god.

Kar-sèr-Sephiryth focused his thoughts on the sword. He was surprised to find it nearby.

*

A gusting wind whipped the Teacher's clothes as he stepped sure-footed through the tent city and into the poorest area of Ezekan. He had been here many times and knew the alleys and pathways well. The nightly aurora had long since faded and dark shadows raced across the twin moons.

The authorities ignored the plight of the poor, most of whom had no means of supporting themselves. Many families spent their nights on the street, sheltered under a bridge or huddled in a blanket on the ground, their meager possessions wrapped in a cloth and clasped close to their chest.

The children had no schooling and were exploited by the merchants and farmers for whom they worked, often from dawn to dusk, for compensation of a mere two meals a day. Kar had made enemies in the Senate when he had demanded better treatment for them, with little result.

He arrived outside the dwelling he sought and with a sense of trepidation climbed the steps to the makeshift front door and pulled the flapping canvas to one side.

He entered and looked slowly around. Sadness weighed on him that some poor wretch would call this hovel his home. A glass of liquor sat on the table. A second lay smashed on the floor, a red stain exploding outward from the shattered goblet.

Something lingered in the room. He felt it chafe his skin like a thousand tiny needle pricks. The sword had been here only minutes before.

Gathering his cloak about him, the Teacher departed Thurle's house and followed the swirl of bio-luminescence left by the sword. He hurried, knowing the trail would fade to nothing before long. He noted the sword's passage through the unguarded city portal and hurriedly climbed the stairs to the top of the outer wall. In the distance, he saw two figures riding abreast. He shivered despite the warm evening. The air crackled with undischarged electricity. Rain burst free of the clouds and thundered earthward. The riders vanished from sight.

Events had been set in motion and could not be stopped. Disparate forces had come together to form something new, or perhaps resurrect something not seen for many generations. The world was on the brink and his time drew near. Urgency built in him, a desire, a *need* to be as one with the sword.

Nine: A Matter of Import

Admiral George Lace paced the floor and waited for the High Reeve to arrive at the "Halfway House," a suite in the Dominion Island spaceport with a modified climate that both Avanauri and humans could endure for a short time, albeit with a degree of discomfort for both.

Yonni's message had been peremptory. "Imperative we meet. Mining operation will be closed down." That was all. No salutations, no valedictions. He couldn't figure out whether the message implied a threat if he didn't attend, or a statement of fact. He hoped it was the former. The crynidium mining plant in the remote Hinterland area had just been established under the management of a local naur and had yet to produce any significant output. It would be a slow process, using local labor and primitive technology, but Yonni would not agree to it under any other conditions. Even so, it was a key plank in the strategy towards full-scale production of the precious metal on

Prosperine.

Yonni-sèr-Abelen was ushered into the room by a human aide. His usual calm demeanor was ruffled. The magnificent speckled blacks around his neck and eyes were even more lustrous than usual, and the fluffy feathers of his mohawk-style haircut stood erect, a sure sign of irritation.

"Greetings, Yonni. Welcome to Spaceport and my apologies—this place isn't ideal for either of us, I know. Will you take a glass of liqueur? It will help you acclimatize." The admiral raised an eyebrow, holding a glass in one hand and a bottle of Napoleon Brandy in the other. "It's 2084, over a hundred years old. Alcohol has excellent pain-alleviating properties."

"Just water," said Yonni shortly, a sour look on his face. "There is a matter of import we must discuss. It would be best if you, too, kept a clear head."

The admiral's eyes flashed, but he maintained his cool. "Help yourself," he said, pouring himself a glass of brandy and gesturing to the jug of water on the table. He placed the drink in front of him, untouched, and sat in one of the two seats.

A half smile played on the High Reeve's features as he fetched the water and eased himself into the chair opposite. "Discourteous as ever, I see, George Lace," he said.

"My apologies if it seems so, Yonni-sèr-Abelen.

Waiting for you to arrive has wearied me."

"Hah!" a guffaw exploded from the Avanauri leader. "Well," he said, "I'm here now. Will you hear my news?"

The admiral nodded.

"I had an unexpected visitor yesterday. The sorcerer, Kar-sèr-Sephiryth, also known as the Teacher." He paused to measure the admiral's reaction. Raised eyebrows seemed to satisfy him. "Can you believe he walked right past my guards straight into my office? He told me an interesting tale of the Sword of Connat-sèra-Haagar. Apparently, an Earth nauri took it from that Pharlaxian *shrelak*, Sequana-sèr-Kira. What was her name? Ah, yes. Hickory Lace." The wispy hair on the High Reeve's head ruffled forward inquisitively, but the admiral looked at him with a stony expression and remained silent. Yonni waved a hand dismissively. "Very well. Let it pass. According to the Teacher, the sword did not stay with her for long but was sent to the Scarf for safe keeping, contrary to the terms of our agreement."

The admiral gave a slight start and sat straighter in his chair. "I was informed of this only yesterday. I intended to tell you today."

"Yes, yes, I'm sure, but here's the interesting part. Somehow, the sword has found its way back to Avanaux!"

The admiral's mouth opened, and the High Reeve rubbed his hands with glee. "Ha! I have you at last. Something you did not know before I did."

"How... You have it?" Relief, mixed with envy, flooded through the admiral.

"George, let me tell this story in my own time. No, I do not have it. In fact, if you believe what the Teacher says it's on its way back to the Scarf." He relaxed back into his chair and raised his eyebrows, nodding his head and smiling.

The admiral could contain himself no longer. He snorted. "Yonni! You don't believe this, surely? A tissue of half-truths and lies. The sword is in the Scarf, yes. My people are there now, searching for it. When it's found, it is my full intention to return it to you—as per our agreement."

The alien's smiled faded, and his eyes flicked back and forth from the admiral to the wall behind his shoulder. After a few moments, he leaned forward and sighed. "I accept what you say. Not all that the Teacher told me can be true. But I believe the sorcerer is in possession of some mystical power. His knowledge and abilities are perplexing. And that is...dangerous. He says if he does not retrieve the sword, a great disaster will befall the world. Liar! With the sword in his hands, he would pose a significant threat to my government, and to your crynidium project."

The admiral breathed more evenly. Yonni was coming to the point.

The High Reeve continued, "I find this naur disturbing. I spoke to him after the battle of Ezekan. It was almost as though he knew what I planned to do before I conceived the thought. He is known to arrive unexpectedly one day, then be found twenty miles away the next. He is feted by the poor and the infirm, and it is said he mends injuries and cures sickness that our wisest physicians cannot heal. Kar-sèr-Sephiryth does not belong in Avanaux. He is almost as alien as you."

The admiral reached for his brandy and took a sip. "You want me to deal with him?"

Yonni-sèr-Abelen grimaced. "I cannot simply have him disposed of. It's too late for that. He has many followers, even some in the Senate speak highly of him. An attempt to end his life would, I fear, spark the very conflagration I wish to avoid." The High Reeve measured his words. "I will not have his death laid at my door."

Admiral George Lace was an astute politician and understood the ruler of Avanaux's meaning precisely. "I have a team of researchers working in the Scarf at the moment," he said. "The Teacher's remarkable abilities may be of some value to them."

Ten: Discovery

Perspiration covered Gareth. His heart thumped erratically in his chest, and he felt the onset of terror gripping his mind. He couldn't move his arms, legs or head; he couldn't raise a finger, regardless of how much he strained. Only his eyes responded to his brain's instructions.

Each day for a week, they had tortured him. The physical agony was like a red hot needle being plunged into his brain, while the psychological torment stripped him of any self-respect, filling him instead with loathing. He screamed for them to stop. He'd tell them whatever they wanted to know. He'd say anything, curse anyone, promise them everything if they would only *stop*.

Three feet above his head, green and orange light pulsed continuously. He turned his eyes down. It took several long minutes for the spots to diminish enough for him to see the dim outline of his body. He was strapped to a narrow bed by a dozen or more metallic sinews. Tubes protruded from different points on his chest and abdomen and were connected to a glass tank of bubbling yellowish liquid. From the corner of his eye, he became aware of hazy alien forms hovering above him and of sharp medical probes approaching his face.

He felt the prick of a needle on his skin and sat bolt upright, eyes bulging. His body trembled with relief as he realized he had been dreaming.

Gareth pressed his hands against the sides of his head, then pushed himself off the bed and poured a glass of water from the tap. He drank slowly, staring at his face in the mirror. He checked his SIM. The simultaneous interpret-telepathic module was an implant that provided for short distance communication and recording. Its most basic use was as a health monitor and chronometer. *Five-thirty am.*

He splashed his face and took a towel outside. The dream had come regularly since his capture by and later rescue from the Bikashi. It always ended the same way, with the injection of the psychedelic drugs that separated him from reality. He rubbed his face with the towel and breathed deeply, staring at the spectacle of the heavens. Both moons were full and seemed to float languidly on the sea's horizon. Prosperine's sun was at nautical dawn, somewhere below the same horizon, causing the moons to be splashed with yellow, orange and red light.

It's so beautiful, he thought, yet alien. He felt

overcome by homesickness, a longing for the peacefulness of his old colonial mansion on Rhode Island where he could sit on the porch and look out over the sea at the yachts sailing past. Jenny would be there now, staring at the stars, even though Prosperine's sun was too distant for her to see.

A dark shape momentarily fluttered by, outlined against the early morning light. *Some kind of nocturnal bat-like creature looking for dinner.* Gareth followed the creature's flight until it plunged into the sea with hardly a splash. He kept his eyes fixed on the spot, hoping to see it surface with a fish, but gave up after a few minutes. He shrugged mentally. *Perhaps the creature is amphibious, or more likely I missed it re-surfacing.*

He decided to take a short walk to the water's edge before going back to bed. He wandered past the wooden lean-to and strolled over the bluff to the next bay with his hands deep in his pockets. The sun edged above the horizon, shining bright and clear.

The tide, having retreated, had left muddy sand rippling outward for half a mile. The conjunction of the sun and two moons must have created an extraordinarily low tide, he thought.

He caught a movement further out and saw the bat creature bolt from the water and soar into the air. He stared at the point where it had broken the surface, then turned and ran to wake the others.

*

"It's not a rock, is it?" said Gareth.

Hickory put a spyglass to her eye, hesitated, and passed it to Jess. "I don't think it's a natural feature at all. The edges are too sharply defined. What do you think, Jess?"

"Interesting," Jess replied. "I'd like to take a closer look. It's heckuva big to be another crashed spaceship. Maybe the top of a sunken city? I agree it's definitely not a natural feature."

"Wow!" said Gareth.

Hickory's brow furrowed. Despite what Jess said, she didn't think something that size could be made from local materials. The most prolific rock on Prosperine was the glistening white stone, carbonatite, used in eighty percent of buildings. This was black and it reflected the sunlight like sheet metal or a synthetic polymer. Could it be of alien origin? "I'm calling the admiral," she said. "We need a boat and some aqua-gear."

*

Adam Brandt took her call. The admiral was in the space station at a meeting with the High Reeve. Hickory explained the situation and Brandt said he would send a crew down as soon as possible.

Hickory greeted the new arrivals as they disembarked the next morning. The leader introduced himself. "Professor Markhov, head

researcher. I specialize in classifying alien artifacts."
He grinned at her. "Which is a *very* specialized field,
given there's not a whole lot of artifacts to classify,
but we're slowly building up an excellent catalog. I'm
pretty excited to hear about your find."

Almost six-foot-six with sandy hair, graying at the
sides, and a close-cropped beard, Markhov was a fit-
looking man in his late forties with an engaging smile.

"Commander Hickory Lace, expedition leader."
She shook hands. "Well, we don't really know what
sort of 'find' it is just yet, but it's certainly unusual."

"I'm keen to take a look. We brought as much
gear down as we could manage. Pity we don't have
an aquasub with us this trip, we'll have to make do
with the Duck." He called to one of his men to begin
unloading the antigrav amphibious vehicle from the
shuttle. "I'll have us ready to go in an hour," he said,
then he left to supervise the transfer of his
equipment from the shuttle.

Forty minutes later, Hickory found him inside
the temporary laboratory he'd erected in the camp.

"I've placed a masking field around the lab, just
in case any locals poke their noses in," said the
professor.

Hickory's eyebrows rose. "That's taking a risk.
Does the admiral know?"

"I couldn't reach him, but I'm sure he'll be okay
with it. Let's face it, we might have a highly

significant alien structure out there in the bay. If we're talking technology, it probably beats anything we've got here—and unless someone walks into the middle of the lab, they'd be unaware there's anything here except beach."

Hickory scanned the range of computer and other technical and testing equipment spread out against the thin walls. Markhov's rationale sounded logical, but she wondered if he'd considered the political impact if the High Reeve ever discovered this breach in the embargo against importing alien technology.

"I'll leave George to handle any political fallout." Markhov smiled at her.

Hickory's eyes flicked towards the professor.

He turned to the entrance. "Everything's set to go, Let me introduce you to the pilot. He'll stay with the craft while we're in the water and pick us up when we're done."

*

The twelve-seater made little noise as it sped across the shore and dashed into the sea. Jess, Gareth, and Hickory hung on more out of habit than necessity as the Duck flew over the tops of the waves.

"The anomaly should be somewhere around here," said Hickory looking at the high-res sonar screen. "It's almost high tide, so it'll be below the surface again."

Jess agreed. "We're on the right line of sight, but we might have come a hundred yards too far, or maybe not far enough."

"We'll pick it up on the sonar," said the professor. "It has a range of four hundred yards. Jeff, let's have a look around here." He motioned to the man at the wheel.

The pilot reduced the throttle, and the craft slowed to a crawl.

Nothing could be seen on the monitor. Gareth frowned. "It might not be that easy to find if it has an aquatic cloak."

"What's that?" said Jess.

"I said if the structure has an aquatic cloak, the sonar won't pick it up." He looked at Jess, who raised one eyebrow. He hurried on. "It's just like the name implies. It's a cool piece of technology developed by other aquacultures. It works differently from a masking field, which is primarily designed to reflect nearby images back to the eye. The aquatic cloak absorbs the multiple sound pings from search equipment. As far as the operator is concerned there's nothing there."

"Nerd," said Jess.

"What?" Gareth shrugged, holding his hands open palm up.

"Enough," said Hickory. "If it is cloaked, is there any way we can locate the target, Gareth?"

"Not unless we jump in the water and swim in circles until we see it."

Hickory sighed. "That's what we'll have to do, then. Get your gear on and let's get moving. Professor, I suggest you anchor here, and the three of us will take a look around."

"No way," said Markhov, shaking his head. "I'm not missing out on the discovery of the century." He pulled the wetsuit over his clothes and adjusted his air supply.

"Look out for the piranhas," said Jess.

"And the butterfly shark—especially the butterfly shark," said Gareth.

The four adjusted their SIM comms implants and slid over the side and into the water.

*

Visibility was good as Markhov's voice came through Hickory's SIM implant. "I performed a chemical analysis on this section of the sea from orbit. The salinity is forty-two percent, which makes it saltier than the Dead Sea on Earth."

Hickory heard her own breathing over the quiet hum of the aqua-propulsion unit on her back. "Spread out, but stay within visual range of the person on either side of you. Keep the chatter to a minimum, but if you spot anything, use the SIM network to alert everybody. Let's go. Half throttle."

The four moved silently through the water at

about ten knots. Hickory took them down to twelve meters then leveled off. Almost immediately, a shout came through from Gareth on the far side of the four swimmers.

"Hey, I've found it."

Hickory propelled herself over to join the other three. Her heart thumped rapidly as the structure loomed into view. Vast and definitely alien in design, the structure had three tiers arranged vertically, each one shaped like the cap of a massive mushroom. A raised platform extended fifty feet from the top like the conning tower of an old-fashioned submarine. *That must be what we spotted from the shore,* Hickory thought.

Fine lines crisscrossed the surface of the top level and electric-blue conduits, as thin as spider crab legs, sprouted from each intersection. The edges of the construct disappeared into the gloom, so from her vantage point, Hickory couldn't tell exactly how big it was, only that it must be huge.

The whole edifice shone like burnished black obsidian, reflecting everything around it. She couldn't see windows, lights, doors, or any other way of getting inside.

Two butterfly sharks swam back and forth like sentinels keeping pace with their reflections in front of the top level. Their eyes swiveled to keep the humans in sight.

"I believe we may be intruding on their territory," said Markhov.

Jess pointed to the lower level of the structure where a school of small fish swarmed, their silvery bodies glinting every time they changed direction. "Piranhas," she murmured.

"I doubt the sharks are too worried for themselves," said Hickory. "Keep your eyes on the surface directly behind them and you'll see why."

Like a magic trick, three smaller butterfly sharks poked their heads out of the shiny black surface then disappeared. Hickory examined the area using the subsonic diagnostic tool they had brought with them. "This whole section is covered in portals of some sort—could be transport bays or other points of entry with a bit of luck. These fish are using one of them for a nest. They're protecting their young ones. "

"Pretty effective camouflage," said Jess.

At that moment, the piranha school swam towards the larger fish. The sharks, with their young in tow, immediately reacted by charging them. The smaller fish scattered as the sharks cut a swathe through them, biting and slicing everything in their path. Blood clouded the water as the piranhas turned on their own.

"Right, let's get out of here. I've got what I need for the moment," said Markhov.

The four swam backward, keeping watch on the

edifice and the fish until they surfaced next to the
Duck.

Eleven: Surprise Guest

The admiral scowled at Hickory from the holoscreen. "You should have waited for me to get back. You're lucky you weren't killed."

"We were in no danger, sir," said Hickory, glancing at Jess and Gareth beside her. Markhov had declined to join them, saying he needed to process the data he had recorded from their trip. Hickory wondered at that: surely he'd want to tell the admiral about their findings?

"Where the hell is Markhov, and who told him to take charge?" The admiral's face burned.

"He's in the lab, looking at the vids from the dive. I assumed he was following your instructions. Is something wrong?" Hickory eyed the admiral. Something wasn't right. Adam Brandt had sent Markhov, and he would have briefed the admiral.

"Markhov is a loose cannon. I'd rather he wasn't involved in this. Did he say anything to you?"

Hickory's hair prickled at the back of her neck. "About what?"

"Never mind. Tell me what you've found so far."

Hickory's eyebrows twitched briefly. She gave her report. "The seismic analysis provides a pretty good picture of the overall shape and size of the edifice. It's big. If I refer to its shape as a triple-capped mushroom, you'll get the idea. The three 'caps' are at least five miles from end to end. Markhov says the black reflective surface is an unknown technology, which is why our instruments didn't pick it up during the regular orbital survey of the planet."

The admiral leaned forward. "So, whatever this is, it's not native. Alien, then?"

Gareth cleared his throat. "Actually, sir, we think it *is* native."

The admiral's steely eyes turned to Gareth. "Go on."

"There's not a dent or a scratch on it, which would be pretty remarkable for an intergalactic spaceship, but then again neither coral nor seaweed has made it their home either. So, yes, it ticks the box for advanced technology, far superior to anything the Avanauri people are capable of, of course. But it's also old—I mean thousands of years old. We've studied the underlying rock structure in the vicinity, and this seabed was dry land not that long ago, geologically speaking. Also, the professor ran the data through PORO, the Proto-sentient Objective Reasoning

Organism, and there are no signs of alien contamination either on the structure itself or on the seabed around it. That pretty much rules out the possibility of it being an alien artifact. And, if we eliminate that, the only conclusion we're left with is that it's native to Prosperine."

"Hmph!" said the admiral. "Eliminate the impossible and whatever's left, no matter how improbable, must be correct. Alright, but, if the Avanauri aren't capable of creating something like this…"

"It has to be the product of a pre-existing civilization. One that's no longer around."

The admiral inclined his head to one side and chuckled. "So, what are you suggesting? A by-gone race that's now extinct?"

Gareth smiled. "Could be, sir. They might have been wiped out by some natural disaster, or war. It is also conceivable that the builders left the planet after they'd completed it."

"Interesting hypothesis, Mr. Blanquette." He turned to Hickory. "Have you figured out how to get in?"

"The surface area on the top level has several entry ports recessed into the surface. We can't tell whether they're accessible until we make the attempt of course, but they look intact, and we're hopeful they're in working order. I recommend that instead of waiting for the next low tide, we go back down there and find a way in, sir."

The admiral pursed his lips and looked at her from beneath his shaggy eyebrows. "How will you prevent yourself from becoming fish food?"

"We can set up tazer-nets around part of the hull. That should keep the fish away, and we can work on it undisturbed."

"Alright, commander. Let's make that happen. Now, you two leave us." He signaled to Jess and Gareth. "I'd like to talk to the commander privately."

*

The admiral's face filled the comms screen. "I thought you'd want to know. I'm bringing Kar-sèr-Sephiryth back with me."

Hickory's eyebrows shot up. "You're what? Why?"

"Mainly because he wanted me to take him here. He seemed to think you could do with some help, and I didn't think you would mind."

Hickory felt the heat rise up her neck. It would be wonderful to have the Teacher here, but she didn't believe for a moment the admiral would agree to bring Kar to the Scarf out of the goodness of his heart. "And?" she said.

"There's no 'and'." The admiral screwed up his face and shook his head. "He seems to know a lot about the Scarf. I don't understand how he could—

even Yonni knows precious little other than rumors. But he may well be of help. He says the sword was recently in Avanaux but is on its way back here."

"What—how?"

"It's a long story. The Teacher can tell you when he arrives."

The admiral knew more than he was saying, and it frustrated Hickory that he wouldn't share it.

The admiral licked his lips and coughed. "On another matter, I want you to stay away from Professor Markhov."

"Why? Are you afraid I might lose my innocence to him? I can assure you, it's too late for that."

The admiral slammed a fist against the desk in front of him. "Dammit, Hickory. Can't you do one thing I ask without an inquisition? Stay away from him, or I'll relieve you of your commission. Do you understand?"

Hickory clenched her fists and shouted. "No, I don't understand. Why are you so bloody-minded? The man's old enough to be my father! And why should you worry about my personal life anyway?"

The admiral's eyes opened wide, and he sat mute.

"You don't have to worry anyway. I haven't seen him since we investigated the anomaly. This whole thing is ridiculous." She folded her arms and shook her head, refusing to look at him.

The admiral spoke so softly she almost didn't hear him. "But, I do worry, Hickory."

*

Hickory's heart beat in her ears like a drum. She watched as the lander settled and the doors opened.

The admiral came out first, followed by two researchers. There was a five-second hiatus before the Teacher appeared in the doorway. He shaded his eyes and looked around the campsite, then lifted an arm in greeting when he spotted Hickory.

Jess nudged her in the side. "Looks like he's pleased to see you." Hickory didn't respond, and Jess looked at her keenly. "Looks like its mutual," she said, "but you'd best say hello to the admiral first, and try to keep your enthusiasm in check." She nudged her again.

"Huh?" Hickory abruptly became aware of the fast approaching admiral, and she stiffened, offering a salute.

"Relax, commander," he said. I know you didn't come out here to meet me. "Ten minutes. You've got ten minutes, and then I want to see you and your crew in my office. Got that?"

"Yes, sir." Hickory turned to face Jess. "Pick up Gareth and I'll see you there in ten."

She walked smartly to greet the Teacher, deliberately ignoring Jess's parting grin.

"Morning, Kar. Did you enjoy your journey?"

"Greetings, Hickory." He reached for her and embraced, then held her at arm's length and gazed at her critically. "You're getting thinner. You need to look after yourself better."

Hickory blushed and glanced at her feet. *Like a giddy little schoolgirl.* She gathered her wits and said, "First time on a flyer? Must have been quite a thrill for you."

"A remarkable experience. I never knew such things were possible, but more edifying by far was to see your people in the flesh. The physical appearance of Earthlings is astounding—such hair!"

Hickory laughed. She felt relieved that he knew her origin at last. They had spent a lot of time together in Erlach, and it had plagued her to keep her true origin a secret from him, although there were occasions when she felt sure there was nothing he didn't know about her.

"I hope our omnivorous habits didn't upset you too much."

The Teacher's eyes clouded over. "I don't know what to think about that. Humans do not have the appearance of carnivores, but your people have gone to extraordinary lengths to keep that aspect secret from the Avanauri. It's worrisome to consider that a race as advanced as yours feeds on other sentient life forms."

"Some experts say the reason we have evolved to

where we are is *because* we eat meat."

"Who knows the mind of Balor, Hickory? It may be as you say; however, it is strange to think this is the way He intended."

Hickory felt a pang in her heart. She sensed his estimation of her had lowered. Who were the more advanced species here? "The admiral says you have some news of the sword?"

"Just as I told him," he said. He related his dream and his conviction that the future of the planet was in jeopardy. "Balor commanded me to come to the Scarf to be united with the sword."

Hickory felt the first flickers of doubt, and it was an ache deep inside like she had lost a precious gift.

His smile was tinged with sadness. "Still, you do not know me, Hickory? At least believe that I saw Thurle and one other flee Ezekan with the sword. And trust me when I say the sword is drawn to this place for a purpose."

She left the Teacher at the door to his quarters and then returned to the admiral's office for the briefing.

Twelve: The Ark

The admiral massaged his temple with his eyes closed. In contrast to his usual military correctness, his uniform was crushed and his hair in disarray. He raised his head and looked at the assembled group with rheumy eyes and a sour expression.

If I didn't know better, I'd say he's had a big night, thought Hickory.

The admiral pulled his jacket straight. "Two days ago, a missing member of our crew turned up in a storage box inside the shuttle. He'd been strangled. There was no sign of a struggle." He paused. "We also discovered some clothing has gone missing. Our forensic people matched the time of death to when the shuttle was last here on El Toro."

Hickory and Jess glanced at each other. They spoke together. "Vogel."

The admiral nodded. "We searched Dominion Island for him, but I'm afraid we were too late. We have to assume he managed to reach the mainland."

"He met up with Thurle, and now he's on his way back here." Hickory's heart was afire. Why hadn't she believed Kar?

"So says the Teacher. We've searched the seas between here and Avanaux and found no sign of either of them."

"Like looking for a needle in a haystack," said Jess.

"They're on their way here." Hickory nodded emphatically.

The admiral's eyebrows rose. "I hardly think we need to concern ourselves with that. If they come near here, I'll take great pleasure in clamping them in irons. Now, tell me about this undersea city you've discovered. How far have you got with finding a way in?"

Hickory pressed her lips together. "It's a slow process. The place is so big. We've identified three possible entry points, though there could be a dozen more we haven't found. Jess has been working with the research team, and she has some exciting news." She nodded at Jess to continue.

"Yes, sir. We discovered a panel with an unfamiliar script located inside one of the alcoves next to what we believe is an entry point. We've fed the script to PORO and had several linguistics experts link in. Nothing of much use, except it's like no known language in the universe. Based on the frequency of some of the glyphs they've guessed there are vowels and consonants, but without a known reference point even PORO is stumped."

The admiral looked at her blankly. "Not what I'd call exciting news, Jess."

"No, sir. But we've also discovered that the sections rotate, clockwise, anticlockwise and clockwise from the top down. It's ultra-slow, but it tells us something is still operational in there."

"That's hopeful at least, but we still need to find a way in."

"Yes, sir. We tried blasting, but our explosives didn't put a dent in the surface. We worked out that the surface is an absorbent micro-shield. We bombarded it with ultrasonics and X-rays, then subjected it to every frequency on the electromagnetic spectrum. Nothing. Then PORO came up with the bright idea of using high-energy gamma rays to create a shower of high-energy particles and antiparticles. The reaction punched a hole in the structure. We've got our way in."

The admiral clapped his hands and looked eagerly at Jess and Hickory. "What did we find?"

Hickory smiled. "Thought you might want to see for yourself, sir."

*

"Prepare yourself, it's breathtaking." Hickory ducked beneath the jagged edge resulting from the gamma-ray reaction and led the admiral inside. The engineers had constructed an airtight nodule over the outside that allowed them to walk the length of the exposed corridor. Hickory slid the door at the end of the passage to one side, and it opened easily. "When we blew the outside portal, we also shorted the internal locks," she said.

This was her third visit, and she still found the scale overwhelming. The door closed behind them, and they walked across a suspended pathway to reach the first of an array of interconnected platforms arranged like a three-dimensional chess board. In every direction they looked, the walls appeared to go on for eternity. "Optical illusion caused by the curvature," she explained. "The shape of this top section is actually a tri-axial ellipsoid. The length from end to end is just under three point two miles, the width is two point four, and the shortest distance," she pointed up and down, "is about one and a half miles. And this is only the top level. The techs have christened it 'The Ark'."

They stood at the edge of a translucent, milky-white honeycomb of interconnected platforms, each of which held a cell, some the size of an Earth skyscraper, others as small as a shoe box, and everything in between. A membrane of waxy threads clung to the walls, linking the cells as far as the eye could see.

Technicians recorded everything they could find; others took samples for analysis. A raft of sensor equipment surrounded one of the largest boxes. "The scientists are hopeful this one houses the operating systems," Hickory said. "We've explored only a small part of the top section, but each compartment we've investigated contains a unique feature. We're speculating, but we think this place is a museum, built to preserve the most important facets of an advanced alien civilization."

The admiral's eyes were wide as he absorbed the scope and alienness of the structure. He nodded slowly. "Or an ark, as the techs so presciently named it. But why build such a thing, and what happened to the builders?"

Markhov joined them. "Well George, the original Ark was created to preserve life on Earth from a natural disaster. Perhaps this was built for a similar reason. I'm hoping the answers to your questions can be found in one of these cells." He gestured vaguely behind him.

The admiral clasped his hands behind his back and jutted his chin forward. "What exactly have you found, Professor?"

"Little more than Hickory has already told you, I'm afraid." He smiled and nodded to her. "There are some items we've been able to identify as works of art and others I'd guess are machines of some sort. I feel as though we should be able to switch them on but I can't figure out how to. I don't know if the power source is missing or if we upset things by blasting a hole in the hull." He shrugged. "Probably the later. We've only cataloged five percent of what's here and we've analyzed a fraction of those."

The admiral's top lip curled upwards. "How long until you've seen it all?"

"Seriously, it could take years. I'd like to figure out a way to dismantle it and take it all back to Earth. We don't have the resources here."

"You know you can't go back to Earth, Markhov."

The professor moved forward until he stood only inches from the admiral. His voice became icy cold. "You don't need to remind me, George. I'm well aware of the consequences. Just get me some more bloody researchers! This is too valuable a find to abandon here."

Hickory glanced from one man to the other. They glared at each other, chins jutting forward, fists clenched and faces red. *What is going on with these two?* Her forehead wrinkled.

Abruptly the admiral broke off and stalked away. Jess looked at Hickory, who signaled for she and Gareth to follow.

Markhov grinned inanely at the admiral's departing back. He saw Hickory studying him and shrugged. "Don't worry about that. It's how we communicate these days. He'll get over it." He smiled at her.

"You must have known him a long time," she said.

"George and I go back a long way."

"Uh huh?" She encouraged him with a smile.

"Yeah. We were in the same class at the Academy."

"Really? What did he mean that you can't go home?"

He clicked his tongue against his teeth and said brusquely, "Sorry, that's personal. Let's just say I'm not welcome on Earth and leave it at that."

But she didn't want to leave it at that. She had an itchy feeling something wasn't as it seemed, something that affected her. She considered reaching out to Markhov with her empathic sense. It wasn't strictly ethical. She had only ever used this capability on an enemy, or when she sensed someone being deliberately and maliciously evasive. Neither of these circumstances applied and she would never use it on a friend or simply to satisfy her curiosity. But the itch persisted and she reached out tentatively.

"Hey! Stop that!"

She blushed furiously and stared at her feet.

"You're a neoteric?" He stared at her incredulously. "Don't you know it's wrong to read another human without permission?"

"I'm sorry. I know there's a connection between us, and I wanted to find out what. I couldn't help myself. I'm sorry, it won't happen again."

"You're damn right it won't. When I say it's personal, it means I don't want to share. Period. Especially with another neoteric. Good God!"

Hickory felt her skin tingle. In her twenty-three years, she had only met two others with talents similar to her own—one of them the Teacher. She looked up at him inquisitively.

His frown smoothed out. He glanced at her, and a grin transformed his face. "Sorry. I didn't mean to snap. You gave me a turn. It's been a long time since I've come across another like me."

"Me too," said Hickory. She had only made contact for an instant, but the connection had been two-way and disturbingly intimate.

He shrugged. "I guess it won't do any harm if I tell you, but no linking of minds, okay? I'd need to get to know you a lot better before I'd consider that." He took a deep breath and continued. "It all happened a long time ago. George and I shared a room, chased the same girls, that sort of thing. The admiral was the serious type. I was a troublemaker, a rebel, hell-bent on stretching the rules. Funnily enough, we got on really well together."

Hickory's thoughts whirled. *Same girl…did he know my mother?*

Markhov didn't seem to notice. His memories absorbed him. "One day I went too far and found myself in trouble with the law. I would have ended up in jail, but George helped me get away, smuggled me off Earth. Years later we met up again, and he offered me a job. He's been good to me, the old admiral. Kept my secret all these years."

Hickory desperately wanted to ask him more about his life on Earth, but didn't want to disrupt his thoughts.

"And then I found out he married my girl..." Markhov gripped the banister so forcefully his knuckles went white. He stared into the middle of the Ark, his eyes rimmed with red.

Hickory almost couldn't speak from the shock. The blood drained from her face, and she felt as though her knees would give way. She tugged his arm. "What...what's your name? Your *real* name?"

He was still lost in his past. "Angela truly seemed an angel come to Earth."

*

"Do you want to tell me what the problem is, or are you going to keep it to yourself until you burst?" Jess gazed at Hickory, her brow wrinkled with concern.

Hickory's eyes flickered. "What do you mean?" she faltered.

"You know very well what I mean. You've been

stomping around the camp for the last couple of days, hardly speaking to anyone except to give an order. Poor Gareth thinks he must have upset you. You've obviously got something on your mind. Are you going to tell me what it is or do I have to beat it out of you?"

Hickory threw her head back and let out an explosive exhalation. "Oh, God. Is it that obvious?" A flush crept across her cheeks. "It's personal, and ridiculous. Are you sure you want to hear it?"

Jess nodded. "Spill it."

"Okay, but you won't believe it, I can hardly believe it myself. You know that the admiral is actually my adoptive father? And I told you what he said about my real father, Jack Manson—that he died in a car accident in New York when I was only two?"

Jess also knew how devastated her friend had been when she found this out, and the lengths to which she'd gone to verify the facts. Many things had clicked into place for Hickory then—the admiral's less than loving concern for her; the gift she'd inherited from her real father. She nodded.

"Jack Manson isn't dead. He's here on Prosperine."

Jess looked at her blankly.

Hickory's throat felt so constricted she could hardly squeeze the words out. "Professor Markhov is Jack Manson. Professor Markhov is my father."

"No, wait." Jess raised a hand and shook her head

slowly. She looked at the ground, before raising her eyes to meet Hickory's. "You're telling me that your natural father is alive and that he's here in the person of Professor Markhov? Hickory! That's marvelous." She jumped up and grabbed Hickory by the hands.

"It's staggering, I don't know how good it is."

"Of course it's good, you stupid girl." Tears formed in Jess's eyes. "I'm so pleased for you. What did he say, what did you say when you found out?"

"He didn't say anything because I didn't tell him. How could I?"

"Hickory, what do you mean? You have to tell him, otherwise…otherwise, oh otherwise you won't be happy."

"It's more complicated than that. I have a horrible feeling the admiral may have set him up all those years ago so he could marry Mom. The professor's already devastated knowing they did marry eventually. He doesn't know about me. Imagine what would happen if he thought the admiral had deliberately…oh, God. It's terrible."

Jess placed an arm around Hickory's shoulder. "If you don't want to tell him, that's your choice. But it might not be what you think. You should at least confront the admiral. See what he has to say." She looked up into Hickory's face and smiled. "Hickory, you have a father!"

Thirteen: Blue Eyes

Hickory's head swam, and beads of sweat broke out on her forehead. Struggling from her bed, she stumbled away from the camp. After a few yards, she could hold onto her stomach no longer. She retched and the contents spewed onto the ground. She wiped her eyes and mouth and inhaled deeply. Something she'd eaten at dinner didn't agree with her. Perhaps she'd unknowingly swallowed a worm or a beetle.

That was the problem with her maquillage-modified digestive system. The Avanauri diet of mostly vegetables sustained her, but red meat in any quantity felt uncomfortable. It wasn't poisonous to her in the way it affected the locals, but her stomach rebelled at the taste of it.

She decided to take a stroll to clear her head and passed the camp perimeter. Five minutes later, she heard something scurry away through the long goldengrass. Her eyes flitted here and there. The only animals they'd encountered on the island so far were small and herbivorous, but that didn't mean there weren't carnivores around. *Probably come to drink at the pool.* She searched the vicinity for telltale tracks, then knelt to examine a mark in the soft ground.

Her heartbeat hammered, adding to the discomfort of her nausea. *A footprint?* Hickory glanced around quickly, then examined the impression more closely. *Five toes!* These were small, like a child's, which meant they didn't belong to any of the researchers. And not Avanauri either, whose feet had four forward-pointing toes. Her mind raced. The footprint looked human. She remembered the Lonilki, the strange people she had met in Erlach. They were human-like in their body shape, but they had the same avian-inherited feet as all Erlachi and Avanauri peoples.

Water seeped slowly into the depression. Soon it would be obliterated, and there would be nothing to show she hadn't been dreaming. She searched further from the waterside and discovered a faint trail of tracks leading away.

Hickory hurried back to the campsite and crammed her backpack with food rations, bottles of water, a hat, her spyglass, some rope and a box of matches. She picked up the belt holding her knife and snapped it to her waist.

"What time is it?" Jess struggled to sit up in her

sleeping bag and rubbed her eyes. Abruptly she came fully awake. "Are you going somewhere? What's the bag for?"

"Go back to sleep, Jess. It's two in the morning. I'm going to have a look at something. I'll be back for breakfast. I'll tell you all about it when I return."

"Sounds very mysterious. You sure you don't want some company?" Jess looked at her obliquely.

She thinks I'm meeting a man. "God, no. But thanks for asking." She gave Jess a wide grin and left the cabin.

*

Hickory hurried back to the pool, praying that the prints would still be visible. Prosperine's moons were partially hidden by clouds, but there was enough light for her to pick up the trail again.

She followed the clues of the creature's passage through dense bush and across the flat land for about a mile, frequently stopping to check the direction. Then the tracks led up a hill covered in long goldengrass, and she lost all signs of her quarry. She climbed to the top and searched the next valley through her spyglass with no result.

El Toro loomed before her. She decided to walk down the other side of the hill before turning back to camp. At the base, she spotted a heel-mark in a patch of damp turf. The print pointed to El Toro. The lower slopes of the mountain were rocky and mostly bare of plant life. It was unlikely there would be more tracks. She knew she should really turn back, but couldn't resist the urge to persist just a little longer.

Half an hour later, she paused to take a breath. As she raised the water bottle to her mouth, she spied movement about two hundred yards ahead. Her heartbeat raced, and she scrabbled to find her eyeglass. She scoured the slope above her, desperately adjusting the focus. *There!* Part of a shadowy head peeped out at her from behind a rock. It ducked away, then came into view again. A hand, half a face and some hair was enough to get excited about. The clouds cleared and she saw the creature's eye was large and blue, and its face and hair white.

Hickory sat and spread out her provisions. Blue Eyes, as she decided to call the hominid, had already shown itself to be timid but inquisitive. She hoped the sight of some edible fungi and dried fruits would tempt it to come closer. Then again, perhaps the hominid was carnivorous and wouldn't be attracted to her meager offering. She nibbled on a mushroom and avoided looking towards the creature's hiding place.

The indigo night sky was tinged with green on the horizon, signaling that daylight wasn't far behind. From the little she had seen of Blue Eyes, she guessed that it must be nocturnal. The paleness of its skin and hair indicated a lack of melanin, usually caused by avoiding sunlight, which meant she didn't have long before it would disappear.

The hominid was too far away to touch with her empathic sense. In the past, she had used her SIM to remove the blocks, patches, and barriers that had been placed in her brain when she was sixteen. This had allowed her reach out over great distances and even control the minds of some lesser beasts such as the Charakai. Hickory turned her focus inward and sought out her empathic receptors.

She sensed the power build within. As she closed her eyes and concentrated, electrical impulses began to swirl around her brain, speeding through her SIM and back to the nerve centers. Her head buzzed, and lights flashed in front of her eyes like a migraine, but she delved deeper until the electrical energy crackled behind her eyes and assaulted her ears and nostrils.

A white burst of power surged through her, and she reached out. The contact was hazy, but it was there. Excitement, fear, agitation, and curiosity; images of others like himself, all white, all blue-eyed, in small family groups. Blue Eyes was a young male, eager for adventure, keen to journey further and further from his clan to discover new things.

A garbled picture of a Bikashi, the most fearsome and intriguing monster he had ever seen, two legged like him but much taller and with a head, ugly and malformed, unfathomable, unlike any other. Except for the one he watched now. Elongated arms and legs; dark face with flashes of purple color; light feathery down like a bird on its head; its whole body covered with strange skins.

Hickory broke off the contact and wiped the perspiration from her face. She reached into her pack, pulled out the analgesics she kept handy, and swallowed two. Her head pounded from the pain.

How ironic that this boy should consider her in her guise as a Castilian to be the alien. Blue Eyes' appearance puzzled her. The indigenous people of Prosperine didn't fall neatly into the species classification system of Earth.

Avanauri were mammals, but they had characteristics of egg-layers like monotremes as well as birds and herbivorous dinosaurs. The Castilieni had a similar genetic makeup, she knew, except that primate genes were present too. Blue Eyes and his family had more pronounced simian features than either.

She wanted desperately to know more, but the sun would be up soon, and Blue Eyes would be gone. She stood slowly, placed several pieces of fruit on top of a nearby rock, then walked deliberately away and back down the mountain.

*

"You are troubled?" The Teacher glanced over

his shoulder as he crouching behind a rock.

"Not really. Not unless you call your whole life being turned upside down being troubled," Hickory muttered. It was the evening after she'd seen the primitive and they'd been waiting in the shadows for hours—too much time for her not to contemplate her personal problems.

She held back her emotion with difficulty. She couldn't honestly believe Professor Markhov was Jack Manson, her natural father. Her father was officially dead. Hickory had seen the death certificate in the central office of records with her own eyes.

To be fair, the professor hadn't actually admitted to being her father, but the story he told about himself, the admiral, and a girl named Angela was too much of a coincidence. Previously the admiral had told her he had married her mother and adopted her after her father's death. Had he lied? Had the records somehow been falsified?

When Markhov mentioned her mother by name, Hickory's mind had frozen, and she'd fled. It was too much for her to take in. She'd gone through twenty years thinking her father was dead. She couldn't just drop it casually into conversation that she was the daughter he'd left behind. "Hi, Dad. Nice to meet you after all this time." Evidently, he didn't recognize her. As far as he knew, she was the admiral's daughter.

Hearing the swish of goldengrass parting, she snapped back to the present, put a finger to her lips and pointed with her free hand.

Part of a face, barely a nose, and eyes protruded from behind the shelter of the grass. Blue Eyes waited several minutes, watching the water hole and sniffing the air before he seemed satisfied, then quickly darted to the edge of the pool. He scooped up several mouthfuls then left his short spear on the ground beside him and submerged a clay pot to fill it with water.

Abruptly, he let go of the jug, and it splashed into the pool. He grabbed his spear and crouched, his head jerking one way then the other, a wild look on his face.

The Teacher rose from behind the rock and walked slowly to the water's edge. He didn't appear to pay any attention to the boy and stooped to drink, then gathered his cloak about him and sat by the bank.

Blue Eyes took several steps backward and glanced quickly behind him.

The boy could flee if he wished, but curiosity held him back. Hickory started as the Teacher spoke in her mind. *Hickory, walk slowly into the open and sit beside me. The boy knows you are here, and he will not come closer if he feels you would harm or capture him. Sitting is a familiar signal of good will and indicates a desire to talk.*

Hickory followed the Teacher's example and sat cross-legged beside him. She extracted a cloth from her backpack and placed it on the ground in front of her, then arranged some sweetmeats on it. The Teacher popped one in his mouth and chewed with obvious relish, then signed to the boy to join them.

The boy approached hesitantly and crouched opposite, poised on the balls of his feet. Hickory pushed a leaf towards him and encouraged him to eat the sweetmeat just within his reach. His eyes widened as he placed the sugar-dusted confection in his mouth. Hickory smiled, nodding at him, and allowed herself her first close look at the boy.

Anatomically, he looked human. His frame was slight but proportionate to his four-foot height. His head was large, with a flat nearly vertical forehead and small brow ridges above two large, round blue eyes. Small pointed teeth sat behind a pair of full lips. His clothing, such as it was, comprised the skin of an animal arranged around his waist down to his knees. Hickory had already noted the pale skin, smeared with earth, and the long, white hair on his head, slicked back with grease. The boy hadn't washed in a long time, if ever. Without thinking, she screwed up her nose.

The primitive stopped chewing and screwed his

nose up.

Remember this as the first communication between your two species, the Teacher's voice spoke in her mind, sparkling with mirth.

Hickory selected another sweet and offered it to the boy on the palm of her hand.

He crouched forward and reached out his arm hesitantly, then jerked it back short of the offering.

Hickory nodded and smiled encouragingly and pushed her hand nearer to the boy.

He shuffled towards her outstretched hand, snatched the sweet, and swiftly moved back out of reach. He put the sweet in his mouth and wrinkled his nose at Hickory.

She laughed out loud and the boy jumped backward, startled.

"No, no," she said. "Please stay. We mean you no harm. Have another." She held her hand out to the boy and tried to project soothing thoughts at him.

Slowly, he came back to take the sweet from her palm then sat down opposite.

"Hickory," she said, tapping her chest. "Hickory."

*

"What happened then?" asked Jess, her eyes wide. She placed a dish of steaming vegetable curry on the ground and sat down.

Hickory ladled some food onto her plate.

"Thanks, Jess, I'm starving. After the sugar fix, he became less suspicious and seemed to accept that we meant him no harm."

"Were you able to communicate with him, Teacher?" asked Jess.

The Teacher declined the plate offered by Jess. "I understood only a little of what he said. The boy possesses telepathic ability, but he seems reluctant to speak. There is a cave somewhere on the mountain where he and others of his kind live. His name is Tirpogh."

Hickory speared a mushroom with her fork. "My SIM couldn't translate, so we talked mainly through sign language. He's very young. He's worried that his family might find out about his nocturnal adventures. I wouldn't be surprised if he's broken some sort of tribal taboo by coming to this part of the island."

Gareth mopped up the last of the gravy on his plate with some bread and grinned. "Sounds like an adventurous little whippersnapper, eh? How primitive do you think he is?"

"Difficult to tell from one meeting. We don't know how widespread his tribe are, or anything about their customs. They might be quite an ancient species. We'd need to examine their culture, talk to some adults from his community." Hickory glanced from Jess to Gareth. "Tirpogh has agreed to take me. Kar has a meeting with the admiral tomorrow…"

"Aaargh," Gareth threw his head back and squeezed his eyes shut. "Wouldn't you know it? I'd love to go, but Markhov practically begged me to work on one of the modules with him tomorrow. He thinks it might hold valuable records of the builders of the Ark, and he needs someone who understands the Schrödinger equation."

"That would be you, boyo," said Jess, nodding her head. A bright smile lit up her face as she turned to Hickory. "Looks like you and me, pardner. When do we head off?"

"As soon as I've finished this," said Hickory. "Get your pack together. The usual stuff, and bring a notebook or something to make a record. The boy will meet us at the pool." She reached across and lightly stroked Gareth's arm. "I'm sure the professor couldn't handle this without you. We'll tell you all about it when we get back."

Fourteen: Troglodytes

Tirpogh's eyes darted left and right, and he clicked and whistled at Hickory and Jess. Prosperine's moons, ghostlike behind a thin cloud layer, bestowed a dusting of dull orange on the boy's hair. After three hours of walking, the land had changed from the predominately grassy slopes to rocky crags. Boulders strewn across the slopes of El Toro cast shadows like dark pools of ink.

When they reached half-way to the summit, the boy signaled for them to wait and scurried up the face of a twenty-foot sheer wall like a mountain goat. His head popped over the top a few minutes later, and he gestured for them to follow.

Jess exhaled audibly, closed her eyes for a moment, then gritted her teeth and followed behind Hickory, placing her feet in the same footholds and her fingers in the same cracks. When she reached the top, Hickory extended a hand and hauled her up the rest of the way. They walked behind Tirpogh along an upward sloping track that clung precipitously to the mountainside.

"Just as well Gareth couldn't come. I don't think he would have managed," said Hickory. Gareth feared nothing living, but heights terrified him.

Two hours later, they made it to the far side of the mountain.

"Breathtaking view," said Jess. She stood on the lower lip of a caldera created by a glacier thousands of years past. White rocks lay inside the crater shimmering radiantly in the moonlight, while the top lip of the caldera was limned with a fiery orange-red from the rising sun.

Hickory nodded to a row of caves running from one edge of the crater to the other. "What do you make of those?"

Jess glanced at Tirpogh who pointed and nodded his head vigorously. "I suspect it's our destination."

Abruptly, the boy threw himself to the ground and cowered behind a boulder. He signaled frantically for the others to do the same.

Hickory and Jess crouched beside him. A flash of movement caught Hickory's eye, then another, and another. Hundreds of flying reptiles poured from the caves and circled in a swarm overhead. The screeching, beaks snapping, and flapping of leather wings grew in intensity until the last creature joined the flock. Almost it seemed at a signal, they wheeled in a circuit of the caldera and flew into the distance.

Hickory scanned the departing reptiles with her spyglass. "I wonder if the Riv-Amok is amongst them." She shook his head. "I can't see him, and I don't hear his voice."

"What are they—Charakai?" said Jess, thinking of the savage bird-reptiles Hickory had summoned to the battle of Ezekan.

Hickory rose to her feet. "No, not Charakai. These are a similar species, but smaller, more intelligent than my friends. I can sense that, but I can't connect with them." After she'd lifted the barriers imposed by the surgeons and successfully controlled the actions of the Charakai, Hickory had discovered that only the less intelligent species were susceptible to her suggestions.

Tirpogh waved for them to follow and set off at a fast pace across the caldera to join a faint track below the caves' entrances. They hurried past a dozen openings where the acrid stink of guano almost overwhelmed Hickory. A hundred yards beyond the last of the caves, Tirpogh knelt and crawled inside a small fissure in the rock face. The hole was large enough to admit Jess, but Hickory needed to be dragged through the entrance by the other two.

"I hope we don't need to come back this way in a hurry," said Hickory, panting.

As they moved further inside, the dim light faded

until eventually blackness surrounded them. A few steps later, Hickory felt the beginnings of panic creep up on her. She stopped with no idea of where she or anyone else was. The air became suffocatingly thick and she could feel the moisture trickle down her neck. Gratefully, she felt a small hand slip into hers. Tirpogh's night vision must be better than her own. After several minutes of total darkness, a faint red glow appeared in the distance. The light drew her on like a moth to a flame.

As the flickering light became brighter, a tumult of angry squawks grew louder. Hickory became aware of walking through a tunnel with walls and roof no more than two feet from her. She forced her claustrophobic thoughts into the back of her mind and concentrated on following Jess and Tirpogh.

A few minutes later, they came upon a porthole in the passage wall. Leaning her head through, Hickory saw a large chamber covered with organic debris; dry goldengrass; leaves; shreds of dry animal skin, bones, and broken eggshells. About fifty young reptile chicks, not yet able to fly, squawked, flopped, and flapped amongst their brothers and sisters.

Tirpogh signaled for Hickory and Jess to wait, leaped nimbly through the gap then tiptoed across the nest, avoiding the snapping beaks of the chicks. He stood silently in the middle of the rookery and closed his eyes.

Hickory's brow knitted as she tried to reach the boy with her empathic gifts. "I don't understand his thoughts, but I'm sure he's communicating with the fledglings."

Half a dozen of the birds flapped over to Tirpogh and squatted before him. He caressed them on their down-covered heads.

"The reptiles will be more impressionable when they're young," said Jess. "Given the way the boy reacted to the adult swarm, I'd guess it doesn't last beyond puberty."

Tirpogh signaled for them to approach and they moved on. Stepping over the nests, they ducked through a small archway into an adjoining chamber. It had become progressively hotter since they'd crawled through the entrance and now they could see the source of the heat and the light. A bubbling pool of molten magma spluttered and hissed only ten feet below them, extending almost wall to wall. Hot, noxious vapors saturated the air.

Hickory took a cloth from her pack and soaked it with drinking water. She gave it to Jess who tied it around her nose and mouth, then she offered another to the boy who looked at it with narrowed eyes and turned away.

They edged around the pool, keeping their backs flat to the wall.

Jess pointed out the marks on the walls created

by previous surges of lava coming from the interior of the planet. "I wonder whether the admiral knows this mountain is a dormant volcano that might explode at any time."

The pathway continued past the lava pool, and they clambered through two smaller chambers until, finally, they came to a dead end. It seemed they could go no further, but Tirpogh approached the rock, turned sideways and disappeared. His head came into view again, and he signaled for them to follow. What had seemed to be a single solid wall blocking their way was an illusion. It was in fact two walls, one behind the other. The original wall face had fractured along a fault line, and a cleft between the two fractured sides had opened just wide enough to let them pass.

*

They emerged onto a ledge, fifty feet above a vast subterranean chamber. Rough stone steps led down to the cavern, which was lit by the flickering flames of hundreds of fires and torches. Jess crouched low, and pulled Tirpogh down beside her, signaling for him to be quiet.

Thousands of half-naked primitives were gathered in the space below, engaged in various activities. Fearsome-looking older versions of Tirpogh, bearded with chalk-white skin and wearing black streaks on their faces, gathered in circles, conversing in their weird language of clicks and whistles. Others oiled spears and axes or took part in a dance celebrating a successful hunt. Females sat apart from the males, some nursing young children or grinding wild seeds on large stone platters while others shaped knives and arrowheads by chipping flakes from stones using handheld tools. Children played games of skill and strength, wrestling, throwing bundles of tightly bound skins to each other or practicing spear throwing.

Jess touched Hickory's arm. "Look there. I don't believe it," she whispered, nodding at the nearby wall. Detailed earth-colored cave paintings depicted hunters brandishing spears at large animals. There were hand prints, images of fire, the sun, the twin moons, and animals and fish presumably from the local area.

Hickory felt a cold tingle on the back of her neck as she came to the picture Jess wanted her to see. Contrary to the previous scenes, this composition had been etched into the rock. There could be little doubt about the subject matter. A triple-capped mushroom shape took center place encircled by three motifs, one seemed to float in the air, another on the sea, and the third had wheels. Dozens of humanoid figures carried crates or led animals into the Ark. "That's incredible," she murmured. Two distinct types of hominids were shown in the etching—the first, and more numerous, were the smaller of the two, who loaded the cargo into the Ark and seemed to defer to the taller lifeforms, who wore helmets.

An excited burst of clicks and whistles interrupted their examination as some of the primitives spotted Tirpogh and his two companions. Warriors grabbed their spears and rushed quickly towards them, while females ushered the children to the far end of the cave and through small openings leading out of the cavern.

Gesticulating and muttering fiercely, one of the warriors bounded up the staircase, grabbed hold of Tirpogh's shoulder and pulled him away from the two strangers. The boy clicked and whistled at the adults, gesturing between the tribe and the newcomers, but he was quickly pushed into the crowd.

"I guess that's Tirpogh's father. Not the warmest of welcomes," murmured Jess.

Hickory's eyes glittered in the firelight. "I wonder if we would do as well in their situation. I daresay we look like monsters to them." The crowd parted as they descended the stairs to the floor, but some of the more courageous young males ran up to them, yelling loudly, and smacked Hickory with their spears before running off.

One of the primitives pushed close to Jess and

flourished a short stick adorned with colored beads in her face. He peered up at her, twisting his head first one way then the other with evident curiosity. He stood at Hickory's side and scrutinized the speckled purple coloring that encompassed her eyes, followed the curvature of her cheekbones, and then faded to a point at her earlobes. He poked a finger at her prominent cheeks and felt her skinny arm. He mumbled something to the primitives behind him.

"I hope they're not measuring us for the pot," whispered Jess. "Do you understand what he's saying? My SIM device is useless. I'm getting nothing but static."

Hickory kept her eyes on the elder in front of her and replied with a straight face. "I can sense curiosity, fear, possibly even wonder, but no detailed thoughts or meanings. We appear to be in no immediate danger of being eaten, although by the look of it that might not last."

The sweet smell of roasting flesh reached Jess's nostrils as she followed Hickory's gaze. Several hominids were suspended on a spit above a fire in the middle of the cavern. Her eyes opened wide, and she gasped. "Oh, God—they're cannibals." She put a hand to her nose to stifle the smell and struggled to stop from retching.

"I'd say they eat their own dead at least, so I doubt they'd be finicky about eating strangers."

"If anything that makes it worse," said Jess, whose face was almost as pale as the natives'. The elder primitive watched this discourse with a quizzical expression, then he grinned, showing two rows of pointed rotting teeth. He turned to his tribe and jabbered at them, stabbing his finger at Hickory as he talked. Those watching emitted a high-pitched ululation.

"I think he just made a joke at our expense," said Hickory. "They're laughing at us."

Jess grinned nervously at the watching crowd. "What's so funny, eh?"

"I don't think he can make his mind up whether we're male or female."

The primitives half pulled, half dragged them towards the middle of the cavern.

"I guess these ones will decide our fate," said Hickory as they approached a dozen or so males seated in a circle.

Fifteen: Prisoners

The Aged Ones observed the approach of the newcomers in silence. Each wore a prized animal skin draped over their shoulders and their hair, saturated with grease, was piled high and tied in place with a leather thong. Their faces glowed with luminescence—a sign to all of their approaching sanctification. Each was worshiped with the reverence accorded to those chosen to petition the Great One on behalf of the tribe.

Hickory's and Jess's escort thrust them forwards and forced them to kneel in the center of the group.

The hair of the most ancient one towered higher than his companions, and the pall of impending death was stamped clearly on his face. He withdrew a long wooden pipe from his mouth and jabbed it at the strangers, speaking in a halting, high-pitched whine interspersed with whistles and clicking sounds.

A hand pushed Jess from behind, and she sprawled into the dust. Another native seized her hands roughly and bound them behind her back.

An argument broke out amongst the Aged Ones, with finger pointing and fists thumping hands. The leader rose slowly to his feet and glared at the most outspoken, who cowered before him, but continued to frown at the prisoners from beneath his skeletal brows.

The leader signaled to the escort, and they hauled Hickory and Jess to their feet then dragged them towards a fenced area containing three dome-shaped huts located on the periphery of the camp. They were pushed inside the nearest hut and the door secured behind them.

The room was small with no windows and scarcely enough room for both to lie down. The walls and roof were sturdy, made with wooden poles and mud covered by dried goldengrass, and bound together with vines.

Jess dragged herself into a sitting position and wrinkled her nose. "Must be the local jail—sure smells like it."

Hickory shivered. A memory of her confinement in the dungeons of the Pharlaxian leader, Sequana, rose like a ghost in her mind but she shook it away. "That etching," she said. "The smaller beings are portrayed as servants or serfs of the taller aliens, but they had an important function in that society. These cave-dwellers look like the same species, but they've regressed to a state of barbarism." She took a deep breath. "And much as the accommodation here leaves a lot to be desired, I'm sorry to tell you it's only a temporary confinement," she said.

"Cannibals, then?" asked Jess, flatly.

"I'm afraid so, and ironically our Avanauri appearance has probably served to whet their appetite. As Earthlings, we would have been looked upon as gods."

"All the more reason for us to get out of here, and fast," said Jess, shivering. "Stand with your back to me and I'll try to loosen your bonds."

The light shining through the smoke hole in the roof helped, and in a few minutes both were free. Jess tested the poles of their hut, but they were too stiff to bend or break loose. "Perhaps we can dig our way out," she said, raising her eyebrows.

"We should have another look at that mural, first," said Hickory. "Give me a pencil from your backpack." She scratched out a small hole through the mud wall and peered at the etching, which was now much closer. "The Ark sits on land but near to the sea, which conforms to the professor's theory," she said. "There's a butterfly shark and some of those strange amphibian creatures found in the bay."

The amphibians, legs spread wide like frogs and heads out of the water, seemed to be gazing at the helmeted hominids. This was positive proof of a different species responsible for the building of the Ark. She dragged her eyes away to examine the next scene. "Jess, come here. Is that what I think it is?" she said, focusing on the outline of a square with a dozen symbols inside.

Jess squinted through the gap. "It looks like the panel at the doorway to the Ark, and that row of symbols beneath it is the same symbols arranged in sequence." She laughed and smacked her hand on the wall. "It's the combination." A wide grin spread across her face. "And this next drawing is a layout of the inside. And the one above the Ark—what do you make of that?" She turned to face Hickory.

Hickory looked at the etching and inhaled quickly. It couldn't be. "Many years ago..." she began hesitantly. The realization of what the message conveyed sunk in and she sat down abruptly.

Jess reached over to touch her shoulder. "Are you alright?"

Hickory nodded. "You remember your history? Before the world government was created, before the New Dark Age, the world was at war for five years. Weapons were invented then that could destroy not only nations but the whole planet. Thank God they were never used." She pointed in the direction of the drawing outside the stockade. "That looks very much like the blast from a pure fusion bomb."

Jess's eyes closed briefly, and she nodded. "I thought so too, but hoped I was wrong. Surely no sane being would arm one of those. The Earth Government and the IA banned the development of PFB's anywhere in the universe."

"We're talking a thousand years ago, centuries prior to the IA. Before testing ended in 2104, they set off a controlled explosion equivalent to ten teratons of TNT on Jupiter. If it had detonated on Earth, the massive neutron flux would have delivered a lethal dose of radiation to everywhere within a five thousand kilometer radius. On Avanaux, that would be an extinction event."

"So, this is a warning, yes? To anyone who would enter the Ark. The first part of the message is the Ark can only be entered in you have the right key…"

"Otherwise, the consequence of getting the combination wrong is—"

"You detonate a PFB."

Jess's face paled, and she stammered. "B…b…but that was a long time ago! It couldn't possibly still be active, could it?"

A muscle on Hickory's cheek twitched, and she gave a curt nod. "A lot in the city is well-preserved— the lights, door locks, climate systems."

"No…no. It must mean something different. Why would the Ark builders do such a thing?" Jess's face broke into a relieved smile. "No, surely if the bomb were still working, it would have gone off when we blasted the door open."

Hickory appreciated Jess's need to counter each argument, hoping to find an easy way out. But since seeing the engraving, a feeling of doom had hit Hickory in the stomach like a boxer's punch. "As far as your first question goes, I can only imagine that the Ark contains something so precious, the builders would prevent it falling into the wrong hands at any cost. The drawing to the far right looks like it might represent the cargo."

Jess examined the square box containing dozens of hieroglyphic symbols. Straight lines connected it to some of the Ark builders, to the primitives and to the fish-creatures. Other lines joined the Ark to trees and the sun, while many other lines ended without any connection. "I can see the trees and sun may be symbolic of the environment. What about the lines that don't connect to anything?"

"Perhaps they're reserved for animal life and cultures on other places on the planet. If this truly is an Ark with a mission to transport Prosperine and reproduce it elsewhere, that would make sense."

Jess breathed rapidly. "And the booby trap? What's your take on that?"

"If everything else is operational, it seems logical the booby trap, if it exists, would be too."

"If it exists? Do you think there could be another

explanation?" Jess's eyes brightened.

Hickory shook her head. "I can only see four alternatives." She counted them off on her fingers. "Perhaps the Ark builders didn't create the booby trap, but some other intelligent species did so for their own reasons. That would be the worst scenario, because we'd be dealing with something entirely unknown." She continued with her second option. "Perhaps the Ark builders deactivated the weapon after inscribing this warning—possibly because the danger they feared had passed. Or, third, the warning is a bluff to scare people away, or—"

"Or it's on some sort of bloody delay!" Jess's eyes widened. "We have to get back to the camp and warn Gareth and the admiral." She scrambled to her feet and thumped the walls of the enclosure.

Hickory restrained Jess's arm. "Wait. That's only what I think. I might have misinterpreted the message. There could be other explanations. In any case, we need to take all this information with us when we leave. PORO might help us interpret it more accurately."

The blood had drained from Jess's face. She took a deep breath and let it out slowly. "Okay. I have the notebook and a pencil. I'll transcribe it if you check it over with me. But that's not going to help us get out of here."

Hickory put an arm around her shoulder and

squeezed. "We'll need some outside help for that. And I've got the right incentive." She pulled a chocolate bar from her backpack.

Sixteen: At Sea

The Bikashi had remained cramped in his tiny cabin since leaving Harbor Town. Thurle had brought him whatever food and drink was on offer, mostly dried fruit and reconstituted vegetables and a little hard cheese. Vogel despaired of ever sinking his teeth into a good juicy slab of beef ever again, but consoled himself with the thought that in a few days, a week at worst, he would be heading home.

The storm arrived midway between the Scarf and Dominion Island, and he lost what little appetite he had. Thurle brought buckets of sea water into his cabin to clean it, but it was never enough to take away the foul smell. When the ocean poured down the hatchway and flooded under his cabin door, he'd had enough. *No point in staying in this hole if I'm going to drown anyway.*

The captain had trimmed the sails, leaving only the jib, but the *Shivering Serpent* pitched and rolled horribly in the raging seas and howling gale. For the fourth time in as many minutes, it lifted it's prow over the top of a forty-five foot wave and crashed downwards into the trough. The wind attacked Vogel fiercely as he clambered up the companionway. And the hat and the cloth covering his face were whipped over the side. Torrential rain stung his eyes, and he grasped hold of a flapping line, fighting to keep his feet. "Captain! Thurle!" he roared.

The boat careened sideways, and he lost his grip. Staggering out of control across the deck, he slammed into the back of a sailor, sending him over the rail. Vogel grasped hold of a forestay and tried to keep track of the crewmember, but the rain, the choppy sea, and the lurching boat made it difficult, and soon the naur had been left far behind.

"Vogel, are you out of your mind? What are you doing here? You must go below," Thurle shouted into his face.

"I'm damned if I will. I'll not wait in that stinking pit to drown."

"You must. You cannot let the crew or our soldiers see you like this. Come, you can have my cabin—I'll share with the men. Look." Thurle pointed at a glimmer of silver light on the horizon. "The storm is almost at an end. When things are back to normal, then we can let the others into our secret, but slowly, deliberately. Not like this." He shook his head and looked into Vogel's eyes.

The Bikashi nodded briefly. "So be it. But if I

drown, know that I will haunt you forever, Thurle."
The cackle might have been a laugh, but Thurle had
never heard the commander make a joke. He didn't
dare respond in kind.

*

"So, this is our mysterious benefactor? I am
honored to meet you, at last, friend." The captain
greeted Vogel and Thurle as they entered his cabin.
He finished pouring three glasses of wine and
handed one to Vogel. "Come, sir, you may remove
your outer garments. I promise not to faint like a
nauri." He winked and handed the second glass to
Thurle. "Our good lieutenant here has warned me
that you have an ugly face, but there's no need to be
shy with me. I have seen many ill-favored features
borne of battle in my time."

"That may be so, captain, but amongst my own
people I am counted amongst the rarest of beauties."
Vogel bowed towards Thurle.

Thurle choked on his wine. That was definitely a
joke. The Bikashi had discovered a sense of humor.
He glanced at the sword in Vogel's belt.

"Captain, if I may, before Vogel reveals himself,
I'd like to tell you something more of him—"

"Enough of this nonsense. We are not children
here—" The captain tore free the cloth hiding
Vogel's face. "Wha…" He staggered backward a few
steps, his mouth gaping. "What kind of monster is

this?" he said, staring at the alien's enormous head. Vogel's forehead sloped back sharply, and he had no chin to speak of. His lipless mouth sat below a long twitching snout, while his eyes were dark and set deeply in his skull.

"Captain..." Thurle wrung his hands.

"Ha, ha, ha! A rare beauty, ha ha." The captain slapped Vogel on the shoulder. "You may be the ugliest son of a whore I've ever clapped eyes on, but you have a rare sense of humor. Have another glass of wine, and we can talk of your home country and your beautiful compatriots. Then, when we've had our fill, I'll introduce you to the crew. They are keen to hear of this treasure of yours, and to see the famed Sword of Connat-sèra-Haagar for themselves."

*

It took the *Shivering Serpent* a further three days to reach the outskirts of the Scarf. Vogel, Thurle, and the ship's captain spent the time convincing and cajoling the crew and the hired soldiers to accept Vogel as a warrior prince from the East. He had come to Avanaux to recover the treasure that had been lost in the Scarf and claim what was rightfully his, they said. After the initial shock, they all responded to the promise of great wealth and the threat of the sword.

The silvery torpedo shapes sprang from the wave at the bow of the ship, spread their winged fins and flew alongside. Vogel eyed them hungrily.

"They bring good luck, master Vogel, sir," said the sailor taking depth soundings.

"See if you can catch one for me and I'll give you an extra share of the treasure," said Vogel.

The sailor's eyes widened. "Are you sure...sir?"

The crew gathered to watch the Bikashi prepare and cook the fish on an iron grill. He stuffed it with dehydrated vegetables and rubbed it over with salt, then wrapped it up in a large tropical leaf and baked it. They drifted away one by one, muttering to themselves as he sat down and consumed it with obvious relish.

"Thurle, what's the headcount? Do I imagine it or are we missing another soldier?" said Vogel.

The lieutenant looked askance at the fish on Vogel's plate. "You do realize the Avanauri use these fish to fertilize their fields?"

"Only because your stomach can't digest them. Frankly, this is the best dish I've had since landing on Avanaux twelve months ago. Now, answer my question."

Thurle straightened. "Yes, sir. Byji-sèr-Thren didn't answer roll call this morning. Word has it he drank too much last night and may have slipped overboard. Counting the unfortunate loss during the storm, and the two who skipped ship on Dominion Island, we have four soldiers and three crew looking forward to the fight, sir!"

Seven, plus he and Thurle. The captain wouldn't take part, preferring to stay with his ship. "Alright, I want everyone to come to the morning training session. It'll help hone their skill—and make sure that each has a sharp blade. With luck and the sword's blessing, we should arrive at the island tomorrow morning." Vogel's skill in navigating the shallow inlets and narrow gorges impressed the crew, but Vogel knew the sword was drawn to the spaceship lying on the seabed offshore of the Island, and would unerringly take him there.

*

Vogel stared at the beach through his spyglass. There were more people than he had anticipated. *But not enough to worry about*, the sword whispered. Vogel wondered if he were quite mad. The sword talked to him more and more, and as each day passed he become less and less like a Bikashi shock troop commander. Vogel wasn't sure what he was transforming into. The strange sense of humor he'd developed was one shocking sign of how much his brain had changed. It seemed to go hand in hand with an increase in tolerance of Thurle's peccadilloes— he'd actually come to like the naur!

Conversely, he had much less patience with the things he was unable to mold to his needs, like the inferior fighting skills of the naurs, the slow pace of the sailing ship, and the unpredictability of the weather. The crew quickly learned to avoid his company at such times. His temper became legendary. Other signs of the change included how little sleep he needed, and his incredible appetite for knowledge, just as Connat-sèra-Haagar had experienced. He guffawed. *What kind of magic would give a Bikashi a sense of humor and a thirst for knowledge?* He vowed he would regain his usual nature when this had ended.

Every morning, he exercised and practiced battle techniques with the volunteers on deck. He marveled at how strong his muscles had become, the quickness of his reflexes, his sharper eyesight and the improvements to his senses of smell and taste. When he realized he had grown an inch or two in height, Vogel felt that perhaps he would be able to cope with the less desirable changes the sword had brought about after all.

The *Shivering Serpent* lay ten miles from shore, and the enemy were but dots in his spyglass, scurrying to and fro. There did seem to be an unusual amount of activity. He shifted his focus to the hills beyond the beach and saw other figures there. He pocketed his spyglass and stomped off the poop-deck impatiently. It would be at least four hours before he'd be close enough to work out what was going on.

Vogel lay on his cabin bed and considered his options. Another soldier had gone down with fever overnight. That left himself, Thurle, the Captain and five fighters to get the job done. His priority was to escape this planet, but he wasn't about to leave empty-handed. The shuttlecraft on the beach appeared an enticing prospect, but only if he got what he came for.

When he'd discovered what first looked to be a sunken city, he'd paddled his raft around it several times looking for a way in. He'd even risked the butterfly sharks to search underwater, but all to no avail. He'd told Thurle and the rest that there was unlimited treasure to be found there, and he felt sure it was as he said, although it might not be in the most convenient currency for them.

Had the Agency found the city, yet? It was possible, even probable. He had discovered it by accident when he went out to spear a fish for his dinner. He felt sure the clever Earthmen would have found a way in by now. His plan was simple: locate the entrance, kill whoever was inside, strip the place of its valuables, especially any weapons technology, and collect some trinkets to keep his soldiers happy. Then he would sail to the island, pirate the shuttle and fly to the orbital space station. He'd take his chances on finding transport to a friendly world from there.

He shouted for Thurle and issued directions for a change of course.

Seventeen: Looking for Answers

Hickory and Jess sat at one side of the rectangular table. Opposite them, the admiral, Professor Markhov, Gareth and Kar-sèr-Sephiryth listened as the two adventurers concluded their report.

"Tirpogh set us free. The elders were busy officiating at a ceremony before the tribe ate. All the adults were involved so the timing couldn't have been better," said Jess. "We managed to copy down the drawings, then Tirpogh led us out of the cavern."

"How is the boy?" asked the Teacher.

"He's okay. A bit upset at having to leave his tribe, of course. But he realizes there was no choice. He would have ended up on the barbecue if he'd stayed."

"Jess!" Gareth spluttered.

"What? It's the truth."

Hickory continued. "It's an Ark, just as we figured. There's even instructions for getting inside without blowing a hole in it." She unraveled the transcriptions they'd copied from the cave. She pointed out the images of the Ark and the lettering.

Markhov swept the symbols with a mobile scanner. "Let me get these off to the lab. They could give us a breakthrough."

The admiral studied the map and tapped on the figures next to the Ark. "What do you think these represent?"

Jess glanced at Hickory who nodded for her to continue. "It's only guesswork, but we believe the Ark builders left this record behind when their future came under threat. We know from our records that Prosperine's sun entered a period of increased activity several thousand years ago. They would have seen a transformation in everything around them, and I suspect they themselves were being affected.

"They left this on the rock face for a future generation—our guess is they knew those left behind would devolve to a simpler state of being. It had to be easy to understand because it was a warning. A warning to avoid the Ark."

Hickory traced her finger along the drawings. "There's something here that has the appearance of a massive explosion." She hesitated. "I have no proof of what I'm about to tell you, but I think we need to consider getting out of here as soon as possible."

"What? And leave possibly the most significant scientific find in a decade lying here for someone else to claim?" An angry red flush crept up the admiral's neck.

"If I'm right, there won't be anything left for anyone to 'claim.' I believe we've already set the clock running for an explosion that will destroy the Ark, this island and possibly the planet." Hickory's breath came unevenly. She felt sure she was right, but would anyone believe her? She outlined her four alternatives. "It seems to me the most logical conclusion is a time delay, but if anyone has any other insights, now would be a good time to share them." She looked at each of the people around the table.

Gareth coughed. "They'd need to be mad to do it. I think your third option is the most likely—it's a bluff."

"Not one I'd like to call," said Jess.

Gareth nodded his agreement. "It's a risk, and the consequence of guessing wrong is catastrophic, but I still think it's the more likely option."

The admiral put his fists on the table and rose from his seat. "I agree there's a risk, but there's danger in everything we do at the Agency. Before I can pull us out of here, I need to be convinced there is a bomb, and if it's on time delay, how long do we have?"

Markhov gathered his notes and said, "I'd best be going then. The answer has to lie in the script. I'll get PORO onto it as quickly as possible." He half rose.

The admiral held up a hand. "We all need to get

moving on this. Does anyone have anything to add before we break up the meeting?"

Jess said, "One of the drawings we copied, we can't make sense of." She tapped at the map. A picture of a cross sat on top of a hill, encircled by a ring of symbols.

Hickory caught the Teacher's eye. "Kar, you have some thoughts on this?"

The Teacher looked around the table. "I haven't worked out what it all means, but I believe the cross figure is both rational and symbolic. I have always thought the Sword of Connat-sera-Haagar has a role in the destiny of Prosperine."

The admiral stood up, calling an end to the meeting. "If this is the sword, perhaps the professor will be able to shed some light on that mystery too. We'll reconvene when he gets the results from PORO."

*

"We've finished analyzing the symbols from the cave." Markhov slouched in a chair in front of the admiral's desk. His eyes were red-rimmed and his eyebrows drawn together. He pinched the top of his nose between thumb and forefinger and said, "I wanted to give you the highlights before we talk to the others. The crew worked on it all night and with PORO's help I think we've figured it out."

The admiral rested his elbows on the desk and

joined his hand, pressing his thumbs against his lips. "Go on," he said.

"After we completed the preliminary analysis, Jimmy retested the entry panel and discovered an aperiodic electrical spike."

"A what?"

"An aperiodic electrical spike. The computer systems in the Ark are a hybrid of chemical, digital and analog processes. The signals from a digital computer are represented by a sequence of two values—either on or off, or one-zero in binary code. Analog computers, when they were in vogue on Earth, had continuously varying voltages. In the Ark, the pulse streams have been unlocked, so they arrive at arbitrary times. That's why we didn't discover it before now." He paused to allow the admiral to digest this.

"So it's giving off some sort of sporadic signal— like it's only working now and then?"

"The systems have been working continuously ever since they were programmed. No, I'm afraid the pulses only started once we broke through the lock. It took us till now to notice because the signal is transmitted irregularly. George, the point is we've been damned lucky to catch it."

Markhov stared at the admiral's fingers drumming on the table and narrowed his eyes. "We sent the signals to the lab along with the symbols from the cave."

"For God's sake, Jack, get to the point."

The scientist pressed his lips together grimly. "Short answer, it's a self-destruct sequence. This place is set to blow."

Eighteen: The Segniori

Later, in the boardroom, Markhov shared his findings with the others.

Gareth shook his head. "What would make them want to destroy all that they've achieved here? It doesn't make sense."

The professor raised his eyebrows and smiled grimly. "I'm afraid it does. Once we deciphered the code and unlocked their systems, we found numerous records concerning the Segniori—that's what they called themselves, by the way.

"Fifty millennia ago, Prosperine's sun had begun the first stage of a cycle that will eventually lead to it becoming a dwarf star. Its outer envelope of gas began expanding rapidly. Scientists predicted that Prosperine would be engulfed within a hundred thousand years. Of course, the planet would become uninhabitable tens of thousands of years before that. They conceived a grand plan to save their species and their culture from extinction."

The admiral noted the mixture of wonder and

skepticism on the faces of those listening and interrupted. "Start from the beginning, Markhov. Tell us how you know this stuff."

Markhov rubbed his hands together. "We constructed a test environment inside PORO to explore what we thought was a logical explanation for the storage compartments in the Ark. As you know, we've discovered bits and pieces of the puzzle, interesting in themselves but ultimately frustrating because each piece is a separate link in a chain, one small part of a vast three-dimensional jigsaw.

"We were looking for a primary piece of this puzzle, something we could build the complete picture around. We didn't get far until this morning. We input the symbols from the cave that Hickory and Jess discovered. It was like waving a magic wand. PORO immediately told us where to find the primary puzzle piece."

Gareth whistled. "The Segniori must have built in a dark sleuth, and when the symbols were placed in the right sequence, it unlocked the key to their database."

Jess rolled her eyes. "A dark sleuth?"

"A background program that provides an overview of the system architecture to authorized operators—in this case, PORO."

Markhov beamed at him. "Exactly. And the primary puzzle piece turned out to be a visual record of their race, past and present, plus their intentions for the Ark—everything we'd like to know."

"Press the button, Markhov. Don't keep everybody waiting."

Hickory thought the admiral a little terse. Markhov had been working forty-eight hours straight and deserved his moment in the sun.

Markhov flicked a switch to bring the holoscreen to life. "Remember: what we are seeing is a conversion of the original images adapted by our technology so that our senses can understand it, but I think it's pretty close to the original."

The playback began with a 360-degree panorama of an assemblage of Segniori under a massive domed roof covered with elaborate floral scroll designs. The images of the Segniori on the holoscreen were blurred. Hickory could see that they were a slender people, with hunched backs and apparently bipedal. They gathered in groups filling arched alcoves that stretched from floor to ceiling around the circumference of the hall. Each alcove radiated soft light of a different shade of pastel color.

Markhov paused the hologram and said, "The story begins at a time Prosperine was inhabited by an already ancient and spiritually developed society called the Segniori. They were peaceful and prosperous. Artistic talent and prowess was identified early and encouraged. Individuals took delight in being taught skills that allowed them to contribute in a positive way to society. A flat political structure provided overall governance and growth. This is represented in the holovid by the different colors."

Hickory interrupted, "Very idyllic, but that's a lot of different voices. There would be at least fifty different shades of color in this hall. How did they manage it? Wouldn't it have led to a lot of tension?"

"In our culture, perhaps, but the records mention no war and little crime. Every clan or caste had a voice, but major decisions and policies affecting society as a whole were made by three representative supergroups. The Braxit supergroup comprised mainly scientists, those who looked to the future, who watched the stars, who invented solutions and medicines, and the technology that supported society's development and growth. They're the ones in the reddish colors. The group wearing light blue are the Avrachi. They were builders, constructed cities, roads, communications infrastructure and the factories that turned out products for Segniori consumption. The third influential group were the Cruvet, in yellow. These were the artisans, the literary intelligentsia, the clergy, the historians. They're the ones who left this record for posterity."

The camera swung to a group of red-garbed Segniori sitting on a circular platform floating in the middle of the hall. The Braxit seemed to be directing the discussion.

The picture changed to a chart depicting the sun and the nine planets in the solar system, then to a series of complex symbols.

Gareth's eyes flashed over the screen. "These could be mathematical equations. What does PORO say?"

"Right again," said Markhov. "This tells us that the Hydrogen fuel in the sun's core had started to burn out, and their sun had begun to expand, as I said before. The Braxit predicted that the sun's expansion into the habitable zone of the solar system, including Prosperine, would continue over the following 200,000 years.

"Changes to their planet's climate and physical geography were already happening, caused by the irradiation of atomic particles. Tectonic disturbances were forecast to increase over the next few centuries, changing the face of the planet. They projected that life as they knew it would cease to exist within 30,000 years."

The admiral frowned. "So, 20,000 years ago. And the regression is still happening? The current day Avanauri and Erlachi peoples are actually going backward in evolutionary terms?"

Markhov glanced at the Teacher and nodded heavily. "It sucks, but yeah. You're the obvious exception, Kar."

The admiral's eyes flicked around the room, then settled on the professor. They were like blazing fireballs, but his voice was measured. "Twelve months ago, our scientists advised us that the Avanauri species were close to a flashpoint. In a few hundred years' time, these people are supposed to experience massive growth in their brain cells. Now you're telling us the opposite. How do you account for the difference in views?"

The professor shifted in his chair. "They are close to a flashpoint, just not the one we would want to see happen. I checked the earlier research notes. There was a notable increase in gamma wave activity in the research sample that led to their conclusion, but there was also a relatively high proportion of subjects with increased delta waves. I ran a comparison of these against the rate of expansion of the sun's envelope, and the correlation is over ninety-five percent. I'm sorry to say, there is no impending increase in brain capacity amongst the Avanauri."

Hickory felt her stomach sink. She'd grown to love the Avanauri and the Erlachi, to admire them for their struggles to survive in a hostile climate, and for their ingenuity and essential honesty. She had friends amongst them. And Kar...his belief in his destiny and in his God was absolute. She couldn't imagine what he must be feeling now. She placed a hand on his arm and struggled to find the words that

would make things better for him. "I'm sorry, Kar.
I…I'm so sorry. I felt certain you were the first of a
new society—a symbol of the positive future of the
Avanauri people, something they could aspire to.
There has to be a solution, a way to reverse the
devolution of your people. How can this be
possible?" Even as she said these things, Hickory
wondered what kind of being Kar was, if not a
forerunner of his race.

Kar-sèr-Sephiryth's features were unreadable, his
voice devoid of emotion. His eyes glittered as he
addressed the room. "You need not be concerned for
the people of today. The world is as we have always
known it, and nothing has changed. But for the
future, for our children and our children's children,
my heart is set to breaking. How can it be, that the
Avanauri will be denied their place in eternity? It
seems strange if this be the will of Balor." He
lowered his eyes and it seemed that he had finished
speaking. Then he drew in a long breath and shook
his head. His gaze held them all. "No, Balor is not a
capricious god. His will is steadfast. For the sake of
all on Prosperine, I pray that you, my friends, with
your knowledge of the universe, will find an answer."

Tears glistened in the corner of Hickory's eyes.
Her heart soared with pride. Even in the darkest
times, this naur was a beacon for his people.

A sheen of sweat covered the admiral's forehead.

His fingers drummed on the table. "There's no doubt there will be repercussions when the Agency hierarchy hear about this, and I feel for the Avanauri people. I hope there is something we can do, but we can't do anything about it at this moment. Please let's focus on what we *can* affect. And I'm confused. If the Segniori's goal was to fly off to a new home elsewhere, why is the Ark still here?" He looked around, hoping for an answer.

Hickory's gaze remained fixed on the Teacher. "Something stopped them from going," she said.

Gareth inhaled deeply. "What if…what if there were two Arks? The first one sent ahead to survey and establish the new colony—"

Jess broke in. "It's possible—given what we know of their culture, the builders would leave on the first flight. The settlers, the scientists, the artists would join them later."

"A second Ark would carry most of the history, technology, and culture. They might even have planned a third ship to carry the bulk of the citizens. It would be prudent to wait until they received a green light from the advance party before they committed," said Markhov

"You could be right, although, we've only scratched the surface of level one, and that's enormous. Perhaps levels two and three were meant to carry the people," said Gareth.

"But the second Ark never took off?" The admiral broke into a smile and slapped the table.

Hickory felt her heart leap. "They never got the green light. The pioneers never returned, nor did they send word. Perhaps they met with an accident or encountered a hostile species."

Markhov nodded his head slowly. "Yes, yes. That all makes sense. Ark II is fully functional. It could have taken off anytime in the last 50,000 years, but it didn't. Why? Because it needed Ark I to tell them where to go. I'll instruct my investigators to focus on getting access to the other two levels. That shouldn't be too hard now we have the code. If we find that one of them is designed to carry people, I'd be confident that's the answer. I can put this hypothesis to PORO."

"So, how does the bomb fit into this story?" said the admiral.

Gareth's face lost its excitement. "We have to believe all their hopes for the future were tied up in that second Ark. As generations passed and the pioneers didn't return or send word, those left behind would become more and more worried about the future of the species."

Jess agreed. "But they'd still hold out hope that the call would come. They'd anticipate such an undertaking would take a very long time."

"Yes," said Markhov, "but as time passed,

perhaps centuries, they'd notice things beginning to change and they'd want to safeguard the Ark and its contents until the others returned. So, they created an explosive event that would destroy the Ark if it was opened without having the knowledge of the appropriate code. We triggered that with our ham-fisted attempts to blow in the doorways."

Hickory frowned. It didn't sound right. Yes, protect the Ark, but why use a fusion bomb to do it? Definitely overkill. "Why booby trap it with an explosive that would threaten the entire planet?" she said.

The room fell silent. Everyone looked at Hickory, then at each other.

The admiral shrugged. "Does it matter? If it is a conventional explosive, it'll still rob us of a historical find. If it's a PBF, the result is the same."

"Except it destroys the planet," said Hickory, raising her eyebrows.

Gareth clicked his fingers several times. "There's a piece of the puzzle missing, eh? Something happened after the original pioneers left to frighten the ones left behind into using extreme measures. Anything on the recordings, Professor?"

"There might be. Some of the recordings appear to have been made at a later date, but we haven't found anything yet that would shine a light on this."

The admiral rapped his knuckles on the table.

"People! We don't have time for this. We don't need to know why this happened, only what happened and how to fix it. Now, does anyone have any ideas about that?"

Jess said slowly, "If they were as advanced as we think, they would incorporate a way of disarming the bomb in case of accidental detonation. A code or a key."

The Teacher said, "Something that would survive the regression of society. An artifact of immense power that would seek out the company of individuals who would keep it safe until a place and time when it is needed."

Markhov pointed to the hologram. The image of a sword filled the screen, followed by more symbols. "This was found in a later recording."

Gareth spoke for all. "The sword of Connat-sèra-Haagar!"

The screen went blank.

Everyone looked at the professor. He shook his head. "Unfortunately, that's where this record finishes. There should be other visual records—probably an inventory of contents, lists of people and families selected..." He paused, spreading his hands wide. "The sword is the key to something important. There's no doubt about that, but is it a failsafe device, and if so, how would it be used?"

The Teacher spoke quietly, "The sword of

Connat is imbued with power, a magic that draws it in a time of need to this place, to the Ark, like a magnet draws iron. The ancients made this so, and there will be a reason. Perhaps the sword itself will answer our questions." He paused. "I sense its presence. It is nearby."

Nineteen: Good News Bad News

*H*ickory, good news and not so good. Hickory received the call from Jess via her SIM implant. After the Teacher's pronouncement, the admiral had given Jess permission to use the shuttle to fly over the island while the rest of them remained with the Ark. "Go ahead," she said.

There's no sign of Vogel. I don't think he's on the Island. That's the good news, but we have a problem out here. It looks like the troglodytes are coming over for dinner.

Hickory glanced at Tirpogh. The boy sat on the floor playing with a plastic toy soldier the admiral had given him. "How many are there?" she said.

We passed about a hundred of them on the way to our camp. They should reach there in half an hour. They're armed with spears, and they brought their pets with them.

"They're probably upset we escaped, but I'm surprised they followed us here."

Me too. Could it be the boy they're after?

"Might be, but I don't fancy giving him to them if he doesn't want to go." She handed the boy a handkerchief and signaled for him to tie it over his nose to reduce the effect of the fumes.

I've a bad feeling about this, Hickory.

"Hang in there, Jess. Gareth and four techs are back at camp. I want you to protect the professor's equipment for as long as you can, but if it looks like they're going to attack, I order you to take the shuttle out to the Ark."

Hickory signed off, leaned over and coughed violently. She took Tirpogh by the hand and hurried over to where the admiral, the Teacher, and the professor were gathered. Acrid white smoke filled the Ark's flight deck, lights flashed on the panels in front of them, and a blaring siren made it hard to hear. A few hours earlier, a holo panel had materialized above the station they were working on, displaying a sequence of flashing characters accompanied by the jarring discord. It looked like a countdown, but how long would it take to reach zero?

Quickly, she explained the situation on the beach. "I have to go and help them."

"I'm sorry Hickory, you're needed here." The admiral appeared anything but sorry. He looked angry, and he was taking it out on everyone else. He directed his wrath at the chief scientist. "Professor Markhov, I must know how long we have before we have to evacuate. If you can't tell me, I'll order everyone out now. I'm not putting more Agency lives at risk." A dozen or so specialists still worked inside the Ark.

Markhov glanced up from the station he was working on. He wore a mask and perspiration dripped from his brow. He raised an arm to wipe it away. "If you stop interrupting me, I'll be able to tell you in a few minutes."

"Are you alright, Hickory?" asked the Teacher, leaning over to look into her face.

She gasped and coughed again. "I'm okay. This smoke is catching my throat. Doesn't it bother you?" She accepted a mask and slipped it on. She found it remarkable how calm the Teacher remained in the face of the confusion and danger.

"A slight tickle, nothing more," he replied. "Gareth and Jess are safe for the moment."

Hickory didn't bother to question him on how he could possibly know. She didn't doubt him and felt a measure of relief. On many occasions, he had demonstrated his ability to see and hear things others could not.

Markhov's muffled voice could be heard over the din. "Hickory, come here. I need your help. You too, Admiral."

*

The primitives massed silently on the crest of the

hill, a shadowy outline against the deep red light of the pre-dawn. Each warrior carried a reptile balanced on one forearm and a spear in the other hand.

Jess and Gareth stood side-by-side, watching them. The four technical assistants stood nervously to one side, swords in hand. The pilot of the shuttlecraft sat inside his vehicle, prepared to take off should the primitives reach him. The admiral couldn't risk the shuttle being stranded, and he had issued instructions to leave the others rather than let it be taken if it came to a choice.

"They're symbiotic," said Jess. "I guessed as much when Tirpogh collected a couple of the chicks in the cave on the way into his homeland. They speak with each other, and I'm guessing the birds will carry out the commands of their masters."

"Not good for us, then," said Gareth, loosening his sword belt.

Jess glanced over his shoulder and grimaced. "Bad timing," she said. "I hope the others can figure out how to defuse the bomb."

"Professor Markhov's a pretty smart cookie." Gareth grimaced. "I don't think our techs will be much help in a fight."

"Better than no help at all," said Jess. She called to the technicians. "Hey, boys. Come in close. It'll be easier to look out for each other."

The four techs, holding their weapons

uncertainly, joined them.

"Anybody got any experience of combat?" asked Gareth.

The techs looked at each other, then the youngest looking one spoke, "I did a stint with the Reserves before I joined the Agency. Never saw any fighting, though."

"Uh, okay. Anyone else—no?" Gareth pointed at the youngster. "I'm promoting you to corporal. What's your name, son?"

"Jaxit, Robert Jaxit, sir."

Jess's eyes rolled. "Gareth! Don't be a twit."

"Okay, okay—just some fun before we die." He grinned at the techs.

"Looks like they've waited long enough," said Jess, gazing aver Gareth's shoulder.

The elders, wearing their animal skin cloaks and with their hair piled high, had positioned themselves to face their own warriors. Now, all except the chieftain moved to the rear. He strode along the line and raised his spear above his head. He screamed at his followers, frequently pointing his knobbly club at the visitors.

"What do you think?" said Gareth

"I think we're in trouble."

The leader whirled his club around his head three times, and each time his followers responded with a high-pitched ululation. On the third occasion, the warriors lifted their arms into the air, and the reptiles took off, rising like a dark cloud into the early morning sky.

"Here they come," said Jess, drawing her sword free. "Steady, everyone. Protect your face. They'll go for the eyes first. Cut down any that come within range. Their necks are the most vulnerable to our swords. Try to cut clean and keep your sword moving."

The reptiles swarmed towards them, filling the air with their screams. The main body of warriors followed them, running down the hillside, brandishing their spears and yelling wildly. The elders stayed behind, watching from the ridge.

Hickory, if you've any ideas, now would be a good time. Jess sent the desperate message via her SIM, but heard no reply.

*

Hickory blinked the stinging smoke from her eyes and hurried over to Markhov, who stood in front of a large panel with a translucent front. Deep inside, she glimpsed purple sparks of light shimmering amongst a swirling milky-white mist. Three-dimensional geometric elements and mathematical objects, matrices, and strings of hieroglyphics rotated into view, then disappeared. Other wraith-like shapes fluttered in the background.

"This is the central nervous system of the ship,

I'm sure of it," said Markhov. "It will coordinate all the primary systems like engineering, navigation, atmospheric control, life support, and communications. There's a good chance it also connects to the self-destruct apparatus. If we knew how they are linked, we might be able to disable it."

"How do we find this link?" said Hickory.

"From what we've learned, the ancients were a telepathic race who had a preference for working in harmony with each other. When they were faced with complex problems or tried to conceptualize solutions to their needs using first principles, they would use a networking technique to achieve their goals. I'm hoping that we two in tandem with the Teacher might be able to do the same." He paused. His eyes flicked towards hers, then away.

"But, how?" she asked.

"By linking our minds to this machine in a similar way as we do with PORO. When we get inside, we'll have enough mental energy to engage with the computer and our minds should be able to travel anywhere inside the system."

The admiral shook his head. "You're talking about merging your mind with an alien machine, one we don't have a clue as to how it works? At least humans built PORO and we sort of know what we're doing, but this? It doesn't sound like much of a plan."

"It's the only one I can think of that might

possibly work."

"If we're lucky," said the admiral.

"If we're very lucky," agreed Markhov.

"What happens if we're not so lucky?" said Hickory.

"That's the big unknown. Perhaps we set off the bomb, maybe nothing happens. We could already be too late, and the damn thing will go off in the next minute."

"We have three hours," said the Teacher, approaching them with Tirpogh clutching his hands. "The boy has a rudimentary understanding of the Segniori language. All the primitives learn from an early age how to read the stories on their cave walls. I taught him the meaning of a minute of time and asked him to count on his fingers the number of minute intervals on the clock."

"Clever," murmured Markhov. "Perhaps we can add the boy's telepathic ability to ours to help engage the machine."

The Teacher smiled slightly. "No. That isn't possible. The boy is untrained, and in any case, the language differences would prove to be a hindrance."

"Hmm. Alright then. Three hours should give us enough time, but we must make a start straight away. Admiral, you'd best take the rest of the team back to the *Jabberwocky*. If this thing goes up, it'll take half the planet with it."

"Take the boy too, and I believe Gareth and Jess may need some help," said the Teacher. "They're well at this moment, although exhausted," he said in answer to Hickory's unasked question."

"How...never mind," said the admiral, shaking his head.

*

For weeks he had soared over the mountains, deserts and the forests of this desolate land, enduring the searing heat and the incessant plagues of insects to look for his own kind. He would have given up, except there remained nothing else for him to do. He did not have the strength to fly back to the coldness of the Erlachi Mountains, and every time he thought of attempting the journey, he remembered the promise of the White One that he would find his family here. He held no doubt that the White One only spoke truth, and it gave him heart to continue his search.

He almost passed them by, when he heard the tinny, scratching voice call out in terror. He flew down and walked amongst them, and they bowed down in obeisance; scraggly, unkempt, wild-eyed monstrosities, their wings in tatters. They were scavengers, no longer the proud race of hunters they had once been, unrecognizable as his kin. Despair tore at his heart. These were his family? The last of a noble race reduced to mocking shadows.

Instinctively, Temloki knew this inhospitable land was the cause of their demise. He resolved to leave and attempt the return home to Erlach. Better to die in solitude, or free in the skies over the ocean, than amongst these sorry creatures.

Come, we have need of you, my friend. The Teacher's voice resonated in the mind of Temloki. When he heard the summons, he felt half inclined to ignore it, but the White One had a powerful will and he found himself wheeling towards the source.

*

Temloki hovered high above the beach. Below him, a few of the wingless ones were keeping the Solakah and their puny two-legged companions at bay with their tiny metal teeth. He felt a rage burn like fire in his chest at the memory of Ka-Varla, filled with poisonous arrows. But, no, these were not of the Erlachi. He inhaled deeply and savored a faint but familiar tang. It belonged to the wingless whisperer from a far off world, the one who had spoken to him, friend to the White One.

The Solakah were many and, though small, they were tenacious. He had come upon their lair when searching for his own kind and they had pursued him for many miles.

The memory of his kinfolk filled him with sadness, and then anger at his fate. He swooped on the smaller reptiles, and cut a swathe through the legion, knocking dozens aside and seizing others in his massive jaws. He rolled his enormous frame and spun around, heading back towards them.

The Solakah screeched in alarm but recovered quickly and parted on either side as he approached. Twisting one way then the other, Temloki snapped at any reptile within range.

The flock on his left feigned an attack then pulled away at the last second, enticing the larger beast to pursue them. The remaining body of reptiles closed in behind and attacked from below, striking his underbelly with beak and claw. A few struck at the soft place between wing and shoulder, and Temloki shrieked. The enemy had discovered his weakest spot and now mercilessly attacked his vulnerable flesh.

Spying a tar pit below, he folded his wings and plummeted earthward. At the last moment, before he plunged into the bubbling black pool, he spread his wings. His feet skimmed the surface, and he soared upwards. Many of the reptiles who followed his downward spiral could not pull back in time and disappeared into the tar.

Temloki thrashed the air to gain altitude, and the smaller creatures resumed their attack. He screamed his rage, snapping at them and swiping them with his enormous wings and tail, but they continued to plague him. Temloki flew into the desert. He spotted a dry gully and tumbled into it, then followed its course for miles, twisting and turning at high speed to avoid hitting the walls. The smaller reptiles could not keep up with him. He swooped beneath a rock arch and headed out to sea, his belly skimming the waves to prevent any attack from below.

The reptiles pursued him for a mile, then gave up the chase and headed to the shore. Almost half their number had been destroyed, but there were enough left to fulfill the wishes of their masters. They zeroed in on Gareth and Jess.

*

Gareth slashed upwards and sliced off the heads of the first three to arrive. Looping her weapon overhead in both hands, Jess swung it in an arc that separated half a dozen more from their bodies. Corporal Jaxit and the three newly enlisted troopers waved their swords about with little effect. Blood and gore sprayed over everyone as the reptiles fell from the air.

Startled by the ferocity of the attack, the creatures veered away.

Gareth and Jess stood back to back and braced themselves for the next assault.

"It's a strange world, isn't it?" said Gareth, panting. "The last time I saw the Riv-Amok we were trying to kill him, and he was doing his best to kill us."

"The Teacher's doing, I suspect," said Jess. She called to the techs, huddled together. "Get ready. They're coming back."

They didn't have long to wait. The flock circled once, then flew at them. Jess leaped high, spun away from an outstretched claw then slashed upwards with her sword, impaling one beast. Immediately, she swung downwards in a wide arc that severed several creature's heads from their bodies. The reptiles collapsed to the ground, still pumping blood.

Before Jess could bring her sword to bear again, another reptile flew at her, snapping at her face. She stumbled backward from the surprise of the attack. The beast hissed and spat as she dropped her sword and grasped its neck with both hands. "Gareth!" Frantic, she fell to the ground, the creature's wings flailing about her head and its beak stabbing at her face.

Gareth skewered the reptile through the throat and dragged Jess to her feet. "Come on, Mother. This is no time to lie down on the job." The grin on his face faded as he saw Jaxit face down on the ground, unmoving.

Jess panted, and her sword drooped. "I don't know how much longer I can keep this up. Have you any contact with Hickory? I can't reach her."

Gareth spoke over his shoulder. "She's still in the Ark, probably too far from the surface for our signals to penetrate. Besides, she's got enough on her hands." He laughed. "Torn to pieces and eaten by this lot or blown sky high by an atomic explosion. I don't know which I prefer, Mother!"

Jess grunted and straightened her sword arm. "I've told you before," she said, slashing at the first bird to arrive, "don't," she grunted, slicing the head off another, "call me…" Her voice rose to a shriek. "Mother!" She wheeled the sword around her head and sliced at four reptiles within reach.

Gareth laughed, and wiped at the blood on his forehead, smearing it over his face. "I love it when you get mad." He chuckled, then spoke more soberly, "I guess the preliminaries are over."

The remaining reptiles regrouped, hovering over the heads of the primitives. The chieftain shook his spear and uttered a piercing ululation. His warriors stamped their feet, took three deliberate steps forward, then stopped. The chief repeated his war-cry and launched his spear into the air. It impaled itself, quivering, in the ground twenty feet from the defenders. The primitives and the reptiles leaped forward as one, screaming abuse, cheering and howling as they ran down the hill and across the sand between the shuttlecraft and their foes.

"There goes our wild card out of here," said Gareth, as the shuttle rose into the air.

Jess spoke in a grim whisper to the remaining

techs. "Sell your lives dearly, boys. Make your loved ones proud."

The uproar grew louder and more frightening as the primitives approached.

The Riv-Amok swooped. It flew in from the sea, scything through the reptiles to reach the primitives, slashing with its talons, biting and beating them with its wings. Immediately, the remaining reptiles converged on him. He ignored their repeated strikes and maintained his attack on the primitives.

Landing heavily, the Riv-Amok slid along the ground for twenty feet, and crushed a half dozen natives beneath his belly. Catching another in his jaws, he flipped him into the air and swallowed him whole on the way down. He stood to his full height and grasped a foe with one talon, raised him high for all to see and tore the head from its body. The natives broke in terror, but the reptiles continued to attack.

Finally, the Riv-Amok, weakened from hundreds of slashes and cuts, could fight no longer, and his legs gave way under the weight of his gigantic body.

Jess and Gareth had watched the bloody conflict in horror. "He's down," groaned Gareth.

Twenty: Running out of Luck

"The level of radiation and sub-atomic activity in this part of the ship suggests this is the central controller for the Ark. It's an artificial intelligence unit that coordinates the functions of all the other systems on board." Markhov spread his arms wide to encompass the virtual wall. It was dotted with portals, knobs, and black screens. "We have no idea where the best point of entry might be, so I suggest we spread ourselves out. Hickory, you start with that globular module at the left end. Kar, as your gifts are furthest developed, you take this panel in the middle here, and I'll head over to the other side."

"What do I do with it?" said Hickory.

"Frankly, I don't know yet. Start with a simple approach. Place your hands on any of the features on the surface and reach out to the ship's Artificial Intelligence. Then try to find Kar and I inside the machine. All four of us need to be linked for this to work."

"So, we project our thoughts into the computer, and search around until we connect up with each other, and—"

"And in theory, we should establish a three-dimensional connection with every part of the Ark," continued Markhov. "It should be simple enough to locate the self-destruct control from there."

"Simple?"

Markhov smiled ruefully. "Relatively speaking."

Hickory took up her position and placed her palms against the panels. The material felt soft and warm and molded itself around her hands. *Strange sensation. Like kneading dough, except my hands are the dough.* She concentrated on making her mind receptive to the AI, and within a few minutes, she connected with Kar. *Wow! That was fast. What did you do?*

The Teacher's words were as clear as if he were standing next to her, even more so. *The machine seemed to accept me instantly. It was as though it recognized me.*

Seemed. Hickory considered what the Teacher had said. He didn't make speculative comments.

The Teacher's laughter tumbled through her mind like a bubbling brook. *Believe it or not, I don't know everything, Hickory. I admit to being just as puzzled as you.*

Hickory felt an unfamiliar salty taste at the back

of her tongue.

That's the AI connection. The professor is reaching out to us now. It would be rude to make him wait longer.

Instantly the three minds connected. Markhov's delight was boundless. *It worked—fantastic! I confess I didn't expect us to connect quite so quickly. It's a strange feeling—joining with two other minds at the same time, and...wait a second. There! That's the AI, yes? I haven't used my neoteric skills very much, so this is very new to me. It's like there are three people in my brain, and I'm in yours at the same time.*

Hickory placed her hands over her ears as though she could shut out Markhov's babbling. *Calm down, Professor. You're shouting, and it's painful. You need to project more quietly. Try to control your excitement. Pass on only the key points and keep everything else to yourself. You can do it if you concentrate.*

Sorry. Give me a minute to get the hang of it.

After a few moments, Markhov relaxed. *I'm okay now. It'll take a second to find what we're looking for. Can you both focus on my location, please, and I'll bring up a virtual map of the ship's systems.*

The three-dimensional schematic filled their minds. Markhov manipulated it to home in on the area of interest, which resolved into a cuboid, the edges of which pulsed redly. *Damn, there it is, but it's not accessible from here.*

The Teacher spoke calmly. *I have memorized the whereabouts of the self-destruct control. I can take us to it now.*

The three disengaged from the console. "What an experience," said Markhov.

Hickory wondered briefly how deeply the professor had penetrated her thoughts.

Markhov glanced at the personal body computer on his wrist. "Wait, that's…that's not possible." He frowned and tapped the instrument.

*

Temloki groaned, quivering with pain, but he offered no resistance as the Solakah screeched and yelped in triumph, tearing chunks of flesh from his body. What was a little pain to one who would soon feel nothing at all? He'd had a long life, a wearisome and lonely existence, for the most part, an object of terror feared and hunted by lesser beings. It felt fitting somehow that the Riv-Amok would be undone in this manner by such as the Solakah.

He could feel the scavengers settle on his body, squawking their victory chorus. But in the end, he would triumph. At last, he would join with his mate, Ka-Varla, in the realms of perpetual sleep. The name Riv-Amok would disappear from memory, forgotten by all but a few aged foes until they too passed into the unknown.

Ka-Varla whispered in his ear. He opened his eyes, and she stood before him, magnificent, sleek, shining with vitality, her four nymphlets nestling by her side. She sang a song of welcome, of reunited lovers, of peace. Gradually, Temloki sank deeper into his drowsy lethargy, but then he became aware of a change. Try as he might to keep her with him, the image of Ka-Varla faded to nothing. Abruptly he felt his pain return, and Ka-Varla's song became a scream.

Temloki raised his head and gazed about him in confusion. His kinfolk, all of them scrawny, many barely able to fly, some almost toothless, had come to him. He wondered for a moment whether they would feast on him, then to his joy and pride, they charged into the smaller Solakah.

Seeing this new enemy, the primitives turned to the East and fled.

A fierce fire burned in Temloki's chest. Diminished they might be, pathetic representatives of a once great race, but they were still his people, still had the iron will and determination to fight the enemy to the death, and they had come to aid *him*.

They died by the score. Skewered by the smaller, faster, more agile enemy. Their bodies littered the ground, an occasional desultory flap of a wing the sign of one creature holding on to life. But still they persisted, and in the end, amid the stink of blood, shredded sinew, muscle and spilled guts, with eyes flapping from sockets, ripped wings, and dripping strips of flesh, they overcame their enemy and honored Temloki.

*

"According to this, we've already spent an hour inside the machine. It felt like just a few minutes."

Hickory checked her SIM. "I'm the same. Something happened when we were linked with the computer. Time must flow faster when we're in the machine."

"That's disturbing, but we can't deny the evidence of our own eyes. We need to find that self-destruct. Let's go, Kar."

It took twenty minutes for the Teacher to lead them to the section of the Ark housing the self-destruct systems.

It was cylindrical in form and Markhov paced round the outside. "It's about fifty feet in diameter, and at least a hundred tall, I'd guess," he said, looking up.

Kar placed his hands on the wall. "There's a door, almost invisible," he said, tracing the outline with a finger. "And a latch, here." He pushed and part of the wall slid silently to one side. They went inside and after a few seconds, the doorway closed behind them.

Hickory's breath came hurriedly. The inside of

the cylinder was sooty black with inlaid sections of orange, red, green and blue that glittered and shone in an ultraviolet light emanating from the ceiling. Only dim outlines of Kar and Markhov were visible against the radiance.

"Interesting." Markhov clicked his torch on, but it glowed dimly for only a few seconds then faded to nothing. "Hickory, do you have a flashlight?"

Hickory reached into her side-pack and took out her torch. "It doesn't work either," she said.

Markhov's voice shook with excitement. "The walls absorb all the visible light in the room." He pointed to the ceiling. "That's a black light, emitting long range ultraviolet waves. It produces the striking fluorescence from the high mineral content of the inlaid rocks. Beautiful, but it gives us a problem. With no visible light in here, our eyes will have trouble working out what if anything we're actually seeing."

"Wait here a second," said Hickory, as she felt her way around the circumference of the room and back to Markhov and the Teacher. "There's several sharp projections at waist height around the perimeter. They could have a similar function to those on the central controller."

Markov's voice sounded close. "I don't believe the lighting in this room is purely decorative. We need to complete our business quickly. Extensive exposure to this level of UV is deadly."

The Teacher nodded. "Yes, there is danger here for you, but I sense less so for me. You must remain outside while I seek the self-destruct mechanism. When I find it, I will call for you and we can do what is needed."

Neither Hickory nor Markhov wanted to leave, but both realized the sense of the Teacher's proposal.

"Don't forget, time passes more quickly when you're connected, probably by a factor of sixty, so every second you're in there is a minute in our reality," said Markhov.

After they departed, Kar felt his way around the wall until he came to the first protrusion. He laid his hands upon the shards. They parted and then enveloped his hands. A few seconds later, he withdrew and pursed his lips. He reported telepathically to the two waiting outside the walls. "Not here, I think. The next one, perhaps."

"One hour forty-five to go," said Markhov. "We don't have time for too many more wrong guesses."

It took three more attempts before the Teacher said, "This is the one. Hurry, we have little time left."

Hickory and Markhov returned to the room. "Okay, let's link up," said Markhov. "Remember, this will be like the Segniori recordings we've seen.

When we're inside, anything alien will present itself to our minds as something familiar. We're looking for a key or a button or a lever or some kind of switch."

They linked their minds, put their hands into the nodule, and felt an instant connection with the AI.

Hickory stood in a cold blue spotlight. She could see Kar and the professor standing far away. She became aware of dozens of twisting, translucent vine-like tubes extending from the wall and looping themselves around her body, slipping between her legs, around her neck, circling her waist, arms, and legs. Her heart beat furiously, but the vines seemed to pose no harm to her. She peered closely at the tubes. Each contained a swirling gas or liquid. She saw deep red streaks like blood speeding through the spotlight in one direction, while star-shaped orange nodules swam lazily to and fro. They stopped momentarily in front of her face before passing by. *Are you seeing what I'm seeing?* she whispered.

Yes, we all share the same images, said Markhov, *but we don't have time for sightseeing. We need to find that switch. Just over an hour to detonation.*

Hickory drew in her breath. *I think I found it. Over here on this console.*

Tell me what you see, Hickory, said Markhov.

It looks like a dead-latch. There's a key broken off in the lock!

I was afraid of that. This can only mean the self-destruct is jammed in the on position. It can't be turned off.

Hickory heard Markhov sob. *There must be a way to disable it,* she said.

Not in time. And we don't have the technology. Remember that what we are seeing here is merely an allegory, a symbol representing alien technology. The real thing is infinitely more complicated. I'm afraid we've run out of luck and time.

Wait. The Teacher's voice sounded soft, yet insistent. *I see something different.*

Hickory suddenly recalled that the Teacher came from a different technological background. A deadlock would be meaningless to him. *What do you see?* she asked.

I see a sword stuck fast in a rock. The hilt of the sword is broken off.

Hickory's head swam. Surely this too was an allegory for something incredibly complex. Connat-sèra-Haagar's sword was created by the ones who built the Ark. She communicated these thoughts to Markhov and the Teacher. *Is it possible? Could the sword be a replacement key for the auto-destruct? Oh God, the sword is the answer after all.*

Markhov spoke urgently. *Both of you, de-link now. We need more time to think this through.*

Twenty-one: Spilling Blood

Gareth and Jess watched the Riv-Amok take once more to the skies, this time surrounded by his brethren. The gigantic creatures circled the battlefield and with a screech of triumph headed home.

"Looks like he's found someplace to belong at last," said Jess. She looked at her hands, covered in blood, and absently wiped them on her jacket. When Gareth didn't respond, she glanced at his face, then followed his gaze. "What's that?"

"More trouble," said Gareth.

Jess ran over to where her pack lay on the ground and rummaged around for her spyglass. "It's a fishing boat," she said, lowering the instrument. "It seems to be heading for the Ark."

"As I said, trouble. We need to warn Hickory and the admiral we've got visitors. Hickory, come in… Hickory, can you hear me?"

*

As the three de-linked from the AI, Markhov

checked his watch. "We've got forty-five minutes to come up with an answer."

"What devilry are you involved with now, witch?"

Vogel's rasping voice hit Hickory like a cold shower. She stared at the figure silhouetted in the entrance to the dark room. His massive frame almost filled the doorway, and the sword glowed fiercely in his hand.

"Vogel?" Hickory gaped at the change in the Bikashi. He was a colossus.

Thurle, his lieutenant, and four nervous Avanauri came from behind him to stand by his side.

Vogel sneered. "I have a mind to kill you, Earth-woman, you and your companions." His eyes played over Markhov and alighted on Kar-sèr-Sephiryth. He inhaled sharply and took half a step back. "You!" A long tongue emerged and swept back and forth across Vogel's lips, then disappeared. "You are hard to kill, magician, but you will not escape this time."

One of the soldiers uttered a cry. "Teacher!" He spun towards Thurle and hissed. "You did not tell me the Teacher was our quarry. I will not lay hands on this naur. He is blessed by Balor."

A murmur of agreement rose from the other three, and they lowered their swords.

Thurle cringed. "Nor did you tell me, Bikashi."

Vogel roared. "Would it matter if Balor himself stood before us? I will take what I came for. I will have my revenge against the Earthlings and my treasure." He glared at Thurle and the others.

The Teacher's eyes locked onto Thurle. "I can help you," he said quietly.

Thurle sneered. "And how would you manage that? By turning me over to the peacekeepers?" He laughed hoarsely.

"I will plead your case with the admiral, although I fear it would mean you leaving Avanaux, forever."

The soldier shook his head slowly. "Why should I trust you?"

"Because there is no one else."

Thurle's lips trembled. He glanced at Vogel, then back at the Teacher. He straightened his back and thrust out his chin. "I will take my chances with the Bikashi."

The Teacher sighed. "Very well, but let these others go. There is no point to spilling their blood."

"Those who are not with me are against me," roared Vogel. He raised the sword to strike down the cowering soldiers.

The Teacher raised his voice. "Let them be. They have done you no harm."

Hickory drew her sword and stood beside the Teacher. She had no hope of overcoming the Bikashi. The sword had wrought a huge change in him. He had grown two feet taller and his chest and arms rippled with muscle. The sword always enhanced the bearer's strength and natural abilities while exploiting their weaknesses. Vogel had been a champion, a highly skilled soldier with the Bikashi. Now his martial abilities would be awesome. She could not recall the commander having shown any weakness. There was no hope, but she would not abandon the Teacher.

A flicker of doubt crossed Vogel's face.

The four soldiers seized the opportunity to flee the room.

Markhov spoke urgently. "Hickory, the sword! It's our only chance."

Vogel growled. He sprang forward, weapon in hand, and pointed it at the Teacher. "So, you desire the sword? You will not have it!"

Hickory leaped between them and swung her blade at the Bikashi. Vogel met it with equal force, and the sword shattered in her hand. Hickory gasped. When she'd fought Sequana, her own blade had remained whole, but the Pharlaxian hadn't the strength of the Bikashi. She drew her dagger and lunged at Vogel. He weaved to one side, grasped her arm and sent her flying across the floor. Her head slammed into the wall and she lay there, stunned.

"Thurle," said the Teacher, "help her."

The lieutenant hesitated. He stared first at Hickory, then the Teacher, and finally at the Bikashi. His face twisted with fear at what he saw. Vogel's usually stolid face was set in a wild grin, his slit mouth curved almost to his ears, and his eyes reflected a mad light. He cackled, and it sounded like the braying of a yarrak. Thurle squealed and fell to the floor, then crawled across to Hickory. Muttering and mumbling incomprehensibly, he shook her shoulder, his eyes fixed on the Bikashi all the while.

"You dare defy me?" roared Vogel. He planted one foot in front of the other and leaned towards the Teacher.

"The world is in peril. I do not expect you to comprehend—I barely understand it myself—but the sword and I have some role to play in preventing this disaster. You must surrender it to me."

Vogel laughed incredulously. He raised the sword and pointed it at the Teacher. "No, I will not give up my sword. It is mine by right."

The Teacher advanced a few feet. "You found the sword lying in the mud where the Riv-Amok dropped it. You did nothing to earn it, but the sword used you to come to this place at this time. You must release it to me." He reached out as if to take the blade and Vogel sprang back.

Kar moved his hand to the left, and the sword followed. He moved his hand to the right and the sword tracked the movement like a mesmerized snake.

Vogel grasped the hilt with both hands but could

not control the weapon. "Is this some conjurer's trick?" he growled, breathing heavily.

"Give the sword to me freely and I promise I will help you leave Prosperine."

"No!" Vogel wrenched the sword away, then yelled in pain as the hilt abruptly became too hot to hold.

The Teacher raised his hand, and the sword flew into his palm. The blade glowed and resonated, emitting a high-pitched note.

"Damn you," said Vogel, wrapping his scorched hands in his armpits. What kind of being are you, that this weapon obeys your command?"

"As well ask what kind of weapon is this that exercises a free will," said the Teacher. "Our futures are linked, that's all you need know. Will you submit to my authority?"

Vogel's eyes were wide, he cast his eyes around and picked up a sword lying on the floor where a soldier had dropped it. "One sword will be as good as another for you," he said moving forward.

Thurle rose from the floor like a spirit rising from its grave. He picked up his sword and advanced silently towards the two protagonists. Closing in on Vogel, he thrust the blade into his back, forcing it inwards and upwards, and then pulling it out, bloodied and free.

A surprised look appeared on Vogel's face, and he

turned and smiled weakly at the naur. Thurle rammed the sword deeply into his gut and twisted.

Vogel's eyes opened wide. He wrapped his hands around the traitor's neck and squeezed. "I am not so easy to kill, kinslayer."

Twenty-two: Triple Alpha

Hickory pushed herself to her feet and staggered over to the two enemies. One look was sufficient. Thurle's hand still gripped the hilt of the sword that protruded from Vogel's heart. His eyes bulged, staring into the hellish grin of his opponent whose hands were locked around his throat. Hickory knelt on one knee and checked their pulses to make sure. "Both dead," she said.

Markhov pulled himself to his feet. "We must hurry. There's fifteen minutes left on the clock. That's ninety seconds within the machine. If there's to be any chance we have to link now!" He stared at Kar-sèr-Sephiryth.

The Teacher held the sword with both hands in front of him and a pearl-white glow spread from the sword to enclose him.

"Kar, what's happening?" Hickory could hardly speak. Fear and awe competed for dominance on her face.

"He's going through some sort of transfiguration.

The sword is changing him. He's becoming something different…something more." Markhov stared in fascination. "Teacher, Teacher! Can you hear me? The sword. We must take it to the machine."

*

Kar-sèr-Sephiryth heard the sword whisper, and its words took root in his mind and grew. The sword sang to him of deeds past, both great and small; of the death of the traitor, Sequana, and of the will of Connat-sèra-Haagar, who remained true to herself until the end.

Many heroes had held the sword for a time since its birth in the forge of the Segniori, and the sword spoke with pride of them all. It murmured of political treachery and intrigue, of mystery, of light and darkness. It spoke of the Segniori and the utopia they had created, of the Braxit who foresaw the danger, of the Avrachi who built first the Arks and then molded the sword, and of the Cruvet who breathed life into it.

The sword spoke of Saarg, the greatest warrior of all, and of the Wargus who came from the stars to enslave the Segniori. It told of the last battle of the Segniori when Saarg and his soldiers overthrew the Wargus and cast them out, only to witness the inevitable slow death of his race.

And then the sword sang of the path of the

Teacher, of his genetic links with the Cruvet. It told him about the expansion of Prosperine's sun and its consequences, and Kar-sèr-Sephiryth realized that the professor was right. The Avanauri were regressing. Inevitably sliding towards barbarism. But every millennium, one like him would be born—a reversion to a branch of the Segniori. The last before him had been Connat.

The sword's song became urgent, it's message imperative. It needed his mobility, his strength, to do what needed to be done. He felt it tremble in his hand. He and the sword must become as one. This was his destiny.

Hickory. You must take your father and leave this place. Go quickly. There are but a few minutes left before this world is destroyed. The Sword and I will do what must be done.

Hickory's mind was in turmoil. She felt frightened and vulnerable, incapable of leaving this alien that she had come to love. *Kar...*

She felt the rough hands of Professor Markhov grasp her arms and drag her from the chamber. She fought to stay, but he was too strong for her. *Hickory, my daughter. You must leave him. You cannot sacrifice yourself. You have friends, people who love you, depend on you. Come...*

She struggled to be free, and then the Teacher

spoke again. *Do not be concerned, Hickory. My part in the story is almost at an end, but the story will continue, and you have a vital role to play. Be at peace and know I will be with you always.*

Hickory slumped limply into the professor's arms and he carried her out of the Ark.

*

In the middle of the black room, the Teacher thrust the sword upwards, piercing the roof. Flashes of ultraviolet light sparked and crackled across the ceiling. The eruption of power increased in intensity, and the sword attracted it like a lightning rod. The multicolored luminescent wall rotated slowly at first, then increased in speed until the colors merged and white light filled the room. At the same time, a high-pitched whine increased in frequency until it became inaudible.

The Teacher's last coherent thought, before the agony began, was that the sword could not defuse the bomb. But he felt no regret; he understood, at last, his purpose.

Bolts of energy surged through the sword and into the Teacher from a dozen places on the control panel. The metaphysical essence of life in the Teacher and in the sword glowed incandescently. The atomic structures of their entire beings came apart for a fraction of a second before they bonded in a new configuration, fused into a new being that knew instantly what was required. Gliding to the control panel, it brought the engines to life.

*

The rocket engines of the Ark erupted into flame and clouds of white smoke. The ship trembled as it separated from the seabed. The three-tiered spaceship emerged from the sea, trailing water and steam. It climbed into the sky and accelerated, gradually at first, then faster as it exited the atmosphere.

From the safety of the shuttle, Hickory, Jess and Gareth, Markhov and the admiral watched until the craft became only a fiery streak. Hickory turned away, her tears blinding her. She couldn't watch. The sword had proven to be the key, but not in the way they had surmised. A flash lit up the sky. She felt Gareth and Jess approach on either side and put their arms around her.

She could hold onto her tears no longer. Her shoulders shook, and she hid her face in her hands. The Teacher was gone, unquestionably dead. She wondered, in the final moment before his life was extinguished, whether he felt any regret. She wiped the tears from her face and breathed in deeply. Kar had done what he had been born to do. There would have been no regrets.

She wondered about her future. Would she return to teaching at the Academy, or would she stay with the Corps? Whatever she chose to do, her life would never be the same again. She would do what she could to convince the Agency to find a solution to the problem of the Avanauri regression, but it wouldn't surprise her if they tried to sweep it under the carpet. The IA would stoop to any level to ensure a continuous supply of crynidium.

She looked at the two men still watching the sky. Markhov now realized he was her father—a final gift from Kar. The other was her adoptive father. She hardly knew either. What were they staring at? Nothing could be left of the Ark.

"It can't be!" Gareth's face was flushed, and his eyes were wide. He turned to Hickory. "Look, on the screen. The Ark is still there."

Her heart felt like it would burst, such was the suddenness of the shift from despair to hope. She ran to Gareth's side, followed by Jess, the admiral, and the professor.

"It's still accelerating. The flash we saw must have been from the transition to near light speed. Zero point eight, now."

"It's heading for the sun," said Gareth. "He's going to crash the ship into the sun."

Hickory felt the blood drain from her face. "Gareth, what's the probable outcome of a PFB being detonated on the sun?"

They all looked at her, and Gareth turned to the

screen, his fingers flying. "At that speed? I…I don't know. The release of helium atoms would be enormous—"

Markhov broke in excitedly. "My God, it might be enough to create a helium flash."

The admiral looked from one to the other. "Would someone explain in plain English?"

Markhov nodded to Gareth. "Go on, son. You spotted it first."

Gareth swallowed, desperately trying to keep the smile off his face. "It's due to something called the triple alpha process. If sufficient amounts of helium get dumped onto the sun's core, it adds to the sun's mass, causing it to heat up. If the core temperature rises sufficiently high, the helium nuclei will get enough kinetic energy to fuse together. In small stars like this one, the triple alpha process can initiate in a matter of minutes or hours. The reaction will quickly spread and the sudden onset of helium core fusion is called the helium flash."

"Gareth," said Jess. "You're being a nerd again. Get to the point, please."

Gareth's hands trembled. "Sorry. Getting a little overexcited here. The point is, this renewed helium burning can last hundreds of thousands of years." He looked expectantly at Jess. "Mother! In simple words, the helium burning causes the core to heat up, which causes the sun to shrink. Prosperine's sun will become normal again for at least two hundred thousand years."

Hickory turned to Markhov for confirmation.

"It's true. Prosperine will become much more habitable. The Avanauri, the Erlachi, the primitives—all the different races will start to evolve normally."

"And they'll have a couple of hundred thousand years to plan their future survival," said Jess, looking at her friend. "Do you think he knew?"

Hickory's face shone. "I'm afraid we'll have to wait for the answer to that question." The Teacher's final words came to mind.

Be at peace and know I will be with you always.

About the Author

PJ McDermott grew up in Scotland. As a schoolboy, he read Sci Fi morning and night reveling in the genius of Asimov, Herbert, Niven, Moorcock, Le Guin and H.G. Wells.

These days he enjoys the fantasy novels of Robin Hobb, George Martin and the modern SF writers, Vaughn Heppner and Alex Weir.

In addition to the Prosperine Trilogy, PJ has published the prelude, Dust and Ashes, which deals with the apocalyptic events 84 years before the first book in the series. It is available as an e-book at online retailers.

Writing as Jacob Carlisle, PJ published the semi-biographical novel, Small Fish Big Fish, and several short stories - all of which have been re-issued under the author name PJ McDermott.

PJ lives in Australia with his wife, Sue, two daughters and grandchildren, Mia and Ryder Patrick.

Contact PJ at: pj@pj-mcdermott.com

Website: www.pj-mcdermott.com

CPSIA information can be obtained
at www.ICGtesting.com
Printed in the USA
BVHW032155251219
567827BV00001B/76/P